THE TRUTH WILL SET YOU FREE

A MYSTERY NOVEL

LANA M. FOX

CONTENTS

THE TRUTH WILL SET YOU FREE

Thirty years ago
  After the murder

"Murderer! Liar!"

I heard their outbursts and saw their angry faces as they pressed towards me, causing me to stumble as I walked up the courthouse steps. The boys who killed my boyfriend were on trial, but the town had turned their anger on me.

My father's meaty fist came up in my defense. "Stay away from her," he screamed. He took my arm. "Don't pay any attention to them, Colleen." It was one of the few times in my life he'd defended me. If he knew what I'd done, he would've beat me himself. I cringed at the thought of all the lies I'd told and prayed no one would ever find out.

THIRTY YEARS AGO.

Before the murder.

The madness started the spring after my sixteenth birthday. I met a guy and fell in love. It was crazy and unexpected and beautiful. We did whatever it took to be together, telling lies and sneaking out, because neither our families, nor the people in our small town, was happy about our relationship.

That cold spring morning at two a.m. I went to meet Jose by the river. The roads were crisp with frost, smoke curled from chimneys of our neighbor's houses as I passed by. I had taken a couple bottles of my dad's beer, thinking I'd bring the empty bottles back and tell him he drank them. He'd never remember if he did or not.

My flashlight illuminated the ground, which sparkled like diamonds even though it was almost summer. I wrapped my sister's sweater around me, knowing she'd kill me if she found out I'd borrowed it.

No cars moved around that early, even though we were right next to the Interstate. The houses were dark as I walked to the river, thinking about Jose, and what we were about to do. The bright moon shone on the water and the edges of the sky were lit up like a mirror reflection of the water. The air smelled crisp and clean like the earth after a good rain.

Jose had said he could borrow his brother's car, and that he'd pick me up by the a. I held the flashlight next to my watch, a gold Timex my mom bought me for my birthday and wondered where he was. He'd never been late before.

I shivered and pulled Helen's sweater closer. I found a place on the guardrail to sit. If he didn't come soon, I'd have to go home, and I really didn't want to do that. I hated everything about being home except being with my mom.

After a few minutes, headlights came towards me. I smiled, relieved and excited that Jose was finally there. I stood up and walked over to meet the car. I couldn't wait to crawl inside and feel Jose's arms around me, pulling me close.

The car stopped in front of me. The front door opened, and my heart sank. It wasn't Jose. I backed away as soon as I recognized the driver, my ex-boyfriend, Larry White. There was another guy with Larry, but he was outside the circle of light from their headlights. They walked towards me.

"Hey, *Chica*, what you doin' sitting out here by the river all alone?" Larry asked, leering at me.

I backed up until I hit the guard rail, the cold metal sending a chill down the back of my legs. "None of your business." The beer bottles started slipping from my cold fingers and Larry grabbed them. I shined the flashlight into his eyes, and he pushed my arm away.

"Corona. Steal this from your dad?" He waved the bottles in front of my face. He had a crazed look in his eyes. What was he on? I wondered. I knew he and his friends smoked dope, but this was something else. Something much scarier. I could smell his sweat and the beer on his breath.

The other guy was Larry's best friend, Steve Perkins. Steve was creepy, his hands always straying to where they shouldn't be, while he tried to get us girls to have sex with him. I did my best to stay out of his way. He grabbed my flashlight and threw it over the rail. I heard it clanking as it rolled down the bank towards the river, hitting rocks in its path. "Waiting for some beaner action, *Chica*? What happened to the boyfriend?"

I tried wrestling my arm from his hold, but he pulled me closer. His breath smelled of onions mixed with alcohol and his rank body odor made me gag. I turned my head away.

"We can give you a good time, baby. You don't need no stupid beaner to give you what you need." He leered at me and I squirmed, twisting around, trying to get away.

"Leave me alone and stop calling him that." My nerve ends were on fire. I looked from Larry to Steve. My dad had taught me how to fight dirty. I knew I could take one of them, could I take both?

Steve laughed. "Why would we do that?" He looked over at Larry and winked. "We waylaid your boyfriend so you and us could have a good time." He laughed and pulled me closer and rubbed up against me. His left arm held me against his chest, while his other hand moved in a circular motion against my breast, squeezing and pinching.

"You two have been meeting out here for weeks. It's not hard to know what you want, *Chica*."

"Where's Jose?" I screamed. "What have you done with him? You better not have hurt him." Tearing my hands loose, I knocked his hand off my breast.

Steve twisted me around and tore open the top of my

dress. He slipped his hand inside my bra and groaned. "I could do you right here on the pavement," he whispered.

"You going to let him maul me?" I asked Larry, gritting my teeth. "Tell him to get his filthy hands off me!"

"Or what?" Larry asked. "You gonna tell your old man? He's drunk all the time. What's he going to do? Besides, he'd probably thank us for getting his little girl away from that beaner."

Steve pulled me towards their car. "We showed him what happens to *beaners* who mess with white girls."

I pulled my foot back and kicked as hard as I could, connecting with his leg. He cussed and moved out of my way. "Come on, little girl, be nice to us and we'll give you something even better than Corona."

"Larry, make him let go of me. Your brother will kill you if you hurt me." I grabbed the side of the car, determined not to be shoved inside. My heart pounded. I knew what would happen if they got me in their car.

Larry shook his head. "Nah, he won't care. All Jonas cares about is Helen. Except when he's with Terri or Meagan or Jenn."

"So how come you like Mex-i-cans so much, *Chica?*" Steve drew out the word Mexican like it was a swear word. "What's wrong with my boy, Larry? He can give you a much better time than old Jose." He laughed, and chills spiraled through my soul. "Hell, we both can. It's going to be a good time, baby." He pried my fingers off the door and pushed me further inside.

I fought like crazy, trying to get away, and somehow in our struggle I kneed Steve in the crotch. He yelped and let go of me. I had to get out of there, get home and inside before they caught me. My sandals fell off as I ran. My tormentors were behind me, closing in. Steve tackled me and we both went down, me bucking and cussing, trying to get away.

"Shut up, you little bitch. You're going to wake up the whole town." His hands were all over me, on my breasts, my inner thighs, and he tore at my clothes, trying to rip them off me. I clawed at his face, scraping my nails across his cheek. He swore and backhanded me.

I screamed, calling Steve every bad name I could think of. He slapped his hand over my mouth, and I bit his finger. He squealed and jerked it away. Lights came on in one of the houses nearby. I heard a man's voice yell out, "what's going on out there," and I screamed, "Help me!"

Suddenly I was free. Steve and Larry took off at a dead run to their car, got in and tore off down the road. I laid on the street, my knees bloody from being scraped across the pavement. My body shook so hard, I didn't know if I could stand up.

The man came towards me in his boxer shorts and tee-shirt, carrying a gun. "Are you okay?" He leaned down and pulled me up.

I nodded. My teeth were chattering, but I managed to say, "I think so."

"Do you want me to call the Police?"

"No! I'm okay, I just want to go home." I didn't realize I was crying until snot dripped down on my lips. I swiped it away and looked down at my dress which was ripped in two. Helen's sweater was torn and dirty. I wrapped it closer around my body.

"Did you know them? I couldn't see them or the car. Were they strangers? I really think we should call the police and let them know what happened, so they can look for them."

"No, please." My voice came out a squeak. "I just want to go home."

"If you change your mind, I'll talk to the police for you. Let me grab some pants and I'll walk you home. Make sure they don't come after you again."

I managed a mumbled, "thank you," but the minute he went in his house, I ran home.

Present Day

I've been searching faces since arriving in Cascade Locks, Oregon. I know it's silly, as if I'd recognize my family even if I came face to face with them, but I keep looking, hoping for the best. Wouldn't it be funny if I ran across my mother in the grocery store? Not likely, but so cool. We could meet and get to know each other.

She would explain why she gave me away. She would also explain the check for ten thousand dollars my grandmother gave her. She would tell me if my grandmother was really my grandmother or just someone off the street who took me in because my own mother didn't want me.

My heart sinks because, really, how can she explain any of this away?

The receptionist who checks me into the hotel slides a keycard across the counter with two fingers as though she's afraid to touch me. I glance up at her. Do I look that bad? I feel fragile like a mirror that's shattered, leaving shards all over the floor. If she touches me, will I splinter?

She takes my credit card and I sign my name for the

room. As I write Natalie Merin on the paper, I notice that the tattoo on her wrist is new. I can tell because it looks angry, but the words, oh, the words—it's a beautiful script that says, *Love One Another.*

True words, important words, and I wonder at their meaning for her as I pick up my bag and follow the bellhop down the hall to my room.

I find wadded up bills in my bag and hand them to the young guy who waits patiently. "Thank you," I say, smiling, willing him to turn and leave so I can be alone.

"Do you need anything?" His smile deepens the blue of his eyes. "Do you want some ice?" He nods at the ice bucket sitting on the dresser.

"No," I assure him. "I'm fine." I motion to the door and he blushes a deep red and stumbles over his huge feet on the way out. He's probably only ten years younger than me, but lately I've felt much older than twenty-eight.

As soon as he leaves, I reach into my bag and pull out a photo I found in my grandmother's desk after she died. I'm surprised she kept it because she never wanted to talk about my mother. I know it's a picture of my mom, Colleen Winters, because she looks so much like me. Same blonde hair and blue eyes. Same determined chin. "We have the same nose, Mom," I whisper. I run my fingers over the glossy finish, then hold it up to my heart for a second before I slip it back into my bag.

My hotel room faces the river. I set my carryon bag on the brown and turquoise bed scarf that decorates the end of the queen-sized bed. Beside the bed there are two end tables and a desk with a dark cherry wood chair. The bed looks comfortable and I yawn and think about throwing myself across it and sleeping for a week. Instead, I walk to the slider that opens onto the deck.

Outside, the Columbia River flows between the banks near the back of the hotel and the other side, which I've been told is Washington State. Everything is green and lush and smells clean, so different from the smell of gas fumes and food carts in the city. There's a small rose garden on the right side of the lawn, and I watch as a family of ducks' waddle across the lawn.

After a while, I go back in and call my best friend to let her know I've arrived in Oregon. Her phone goes to voice mail and I tell her that I've made it and will call her soon.

A glance at my watch shows five p.m., Oregon time. Exhaustion tugs at me, but I know I don't have a lot of time in Cascade Locks to find my birth mother and I need to make every minute count. Classes will be starting in about ten days back in Florida, and I have to be there to teach my high schoolers the fine art of the English language.

The next morning, I wake up ready to begin my search. I've made a list of things to do while I'm in Cascade Locks. The first thing is to call Alice Perkins, an old friend of my grand-mother who lives here. I want to show her the picture of Colleen and have her confirm that it is a picture of my mother. After I talk to her, I'm going to find everyone in town who might've known Colleen.

I flip through the contacts in my iPhone and find her number. Alice visited us in Florida years ago. I remember her as a short, round woman with crinkly blonde hair that she wore in a long braid. She reminded me of a Cabbage Patch doll that I had when I was little.

I touch her number on the screen and after a couple rings I hear her voice, faint with age. "Hello? Hello, hello?" I wonder how much she's changed in the years since I saw her.

"Alice, this is Natalie ."

"Who?"

"Natalie , Leona's granddaughter." I choke on the title, but that's how she knows me. All my life I've thought I was Leona's granddaughter.

"I'm sorry...I can't hear so well..." *Click*.

I look at my phone and frown, then I touch the number again. This time it rings and rings and no one answers.

That's so strange. I called Alice before I left Florida to tell her I'd be in Oregon for a few weeks. We had a great visit. She wanted to know how I was doing, how Leona's memorial service went. She had wanted to be there, she said, but she didn't like to fly anymore.

I try her number again with the same result. Since I have her address, which I found in Leona's things, I decide to go to her house. I pull up the google map on my phone and find that her house is only three blocks from the hotel. This town is so tiny, it looks like everything is only three blocks away.

My stomach flutters as I walk to her house. I'm sure she knows about my birth mother. After all, according to my real birth certificate, the one I found after Leona died, my mother was from here.

Grandmother told me that my birth mother, Colleen Winters, died in a car accident when I was a baby. According to the information I found online, Colleen was alive and living in Cascade Locks until twenty years ago. What's with that? I wonder.

I want to find out the truth. Who is this woman who gave me birth then gave me up? Why did she give me up? And why did Leona take me to Florida and lie about my mother?

As I walk from the hotel to the street where Alice lives,

I look around at the charming small town. It's such a change from the big city where I grew up. Cascade Locks is about forty miles from Portland, the biggest city in Oregon. There's one main street and from what I read; the population is 1,148 residents. Although, since it's summer there are lots of people milling about town, talking on the sidewalk, or riding bikes and jogging along the waterfront.

The sun is bright in the sky and warm on my back as I walk to Alice's house. I breathe in the clean air and wish I were here for a vacation with friends. Hannah would love it here. Before I left home, we talked about how much fun it would be to take the Stern Wheeler on a cruise down the Columbia River.

We were sitting in her living room, pouring over the information on Cascade Locks on my laptop. Hannah leaned over her stomach, trying to see the screen over her swelling baby bump.

Now as I walk, I look out at the river. Its allure is almost as great as the Cascade Mountains surrounding us. I stop and watch the boats as they zip along pulling water skiers, windsurfers and kite boarders, their bright sails beautiful against the backdrop of this magical place. A sense of well-being flows over me, and I smile, feeling sure I'll find the answers I'm seeking here. After all, if this part of Oregon is as magical as it looks, anything can happen. Right?

There are several people walking up and down the main road, their voices and laughter swirl around me. The door to a pizza restaurant opens and the smell of garlic and spices makes my stomach growl. They must be getting ready for lunch. I remember I haven't eaten yet today.

Alice's house is small and run down. She calls out a feeble, "come in," when I knock on her door. The door groans and sticks, and I lift it up, so I can slip inside. Alice sits in the living room in her chair, an old recliner that's seen better days. She doesn't get up, just sits and stares at me. A flash of terror crosses her face causing me to catch my breath. It's gone so fast I wonder if I imagined it.

My memories of Alice don't mesh with the tiny old woman I see before me. I was probably eight or nine when I first met her. Twenty years ago, Alice was still strong and lively. She wasn't much taller than me. I remember she and Grandmother loved to take walks and I thought they looked funny together. Grandmother, tall, slim, and elegant, and Alice with her short, round frame and stubby legs. They would take me with them, then we'd go home, and they'd talk late into the night, their voices rising and falling like the volume of a television commercial.

Now her face is creased with wrinkles and her wispy white hair is pulled back into a bun with bits of fluff sticking out all over her head. I look around and think, *hoarder*. Every surface in her home is piled with old magazines and newspapers. There are stacks of books leaning haphazardly around the edges of the room, on the coffee and end tables and spilling out of the bookcase behind the sofa where Alice sits. The English teacher in me wants to pick them up, dust them off and give them to a library. Trash of every kind, from old MacDonald's wrappers to junk mail, to empty Coke boxes litter the floor and clothes and blankets are slung over furniture. The smell of must and filth is so strong I want to pull my shirt up over my nose.

It's hard to think of my grandmother visiting Alice here. Leona was always so fastidious, something she did her best to pass on to me. She needed to have things in order, almost like it was an obsession. How could she have stayed in this house? She would have gone nuts. I know she visited when I was young because I remember staying with the neighbor.

"Natalie?"

I nod and look around for somewhere to sit, but everything is covered. I remove towels and newspapers and finally find the dirty quilt she threw over the sofa. Gingerly, I sit down; thankful I'm wearing jeans, hoping the grime won't filter through to my skin. I don't want to touch anything I don't have to, so I put my hands in my lap.

Alice looks at me through thick glasses. Her eyes are huge from the magnification and look unworldly, as though I'm talking to someone from outer space. I don't see much about her that's recognizable except for her round body, and even that has gotten smaller. "You shouldn't have come here," she whispers. If possible, her eyes get even bigger. "It's not safe."

"Why not?" I look around wondering if the house is going to fall in on us. Surely, she wouldn't be living here if she thought it would.

"Trust me, Natalie. You must go back to Florida. Don't look for Colleen." She motions me to the door with a sweep of her hands.

I turn towards her and hear paper crinkle under my feet. Looking down, I notice that my sandals are resting on a torn newspaper. "Why shouldn't I look for her?"

Alice raises a frail hand and pushes the wispy hair back off her forehead. She shakes her head. "She's gone. Now, please leave before it's too late."

"Too late for what? Why are you afraid of me finding her?" I lean down and take the picture out of my bag.

Alice holds up her hand as though to warn me off. "You don't understand. I don't know where she is and it's better that way."

I move closer to her and place the picture in her hand.

She gasps. Her hand shakes, and she tries to give it back to me.

"Is that her? Is that my mother?"

Alice tilts her head. "I can't see so good. It sorts of looks like her, but it's been so long." She curls her fingers over the picture and right before she crumples it, I grab it out of her hand and slip the picture back into my bag.

"Please tell me why Leona took me and moved to Florida and lied about where I was born." I hear the desperation in my voice and Alice must too because she relents a little.

"She wanted to get you out of here." She puts her fingers over her mouth, like she thinks she can keep the words from tumbling out.

"Why? Didn't I have other family here? What about my grandparents?"

Alice touches the bun on the back of her head. Her eyes are open, but she's not seeing anything in the room. She's looking back in time. "They died a long time ago. It was better that way."

"Better for who?" Not for me, although I didn't have a bad childhood, I didn't have the one I wanted. I felt cheated because my parents were dead, and I didn't have a brother or sister. "Do you know why Colleen gave me up for adoption? Did Leona adopt me? Or did she falsify the adoption papers like she did my birth certificate?"

Alice ignores the disgust that colors my words. "Did your grandmother tell you anything about Colleen?" There's something in her voice that makes me pay attention.

"My grandmother," I stiffen my spine when I talk about her, "said she died when I was a baby. But you and I both know that isn't true. I Googled her. She lived here in

Cascade Locks until I was eight, and then it's like she dropped off the face of the earth. What happened?"

Alice leans back in her chair and rubs her eyes behind the thick frames. "I don't know. She just disappeared. No one knew what happened to her, and no one cared."

This last is said so softly, I almost don't catch it. "Why wouldn't they care? Didn't she have family who wanted to know where she went? This is a small town; didn't she have friends who wondered where she was?"

Alice shakes her head, a faraway look in her eyes. "She wasn't well liked here, Natalie. I know you have some romantic vision of a nice woman who had a baby and for some unfortunate reason had to give her up for adoption. That's not what happened."

"Then what did happen? Tell me so I can understand." I'm so frustrated I want to squeeze the truth out of her. "Did Colleen sell me to Leona for ten-thousand dollars?"

A vein on Alice's forehead pops out. "What are you talking about? I don't know anything about ten-thousand dollars."

"I saw the canceled check, Alice. Leona sent Colleen a check for ten-thousand dollars right after I was born."

"You don't understand. Some things are better left in the past." She takes off her glasses and rubs her eyes. "I'm so tired. I need to lie down."

There's silence in the old house, and I'm so tuned into what I need to find out from her that I almost don't hear the knock on the door. Alice blinks, looking relieved.

"Can you get that? It takes me so long to get up these days."

I jump up and open the door. Two nice looking older ladies walk in carrying casserole dishes filled with something that smells wonderful.

"Oh hey, I didn't know Alice had company. We brought her a meal." One of the gray-haired ladies leans closer to me and whispers, "she wouldn't eat anything but candy bars if we didn't." Then she raises her voice. "Hi Alice, we brought you the cheese enchiladas you love. I'll just set them in the kitchen. They're nice and hot so you can eat whenever you'd like."

The aroma of refried beans and cheese fills the air and my stomach growls, and the other gray-haired lady smiles. "Maybe you can share with this young lady." She sticks out her hand, the one that isn't loaded with groceries. "I'm Marie Collins. And you are?"

Before I can tell her my name, Alice says, "She's leaving." Her eyes drill into mine. "As you can see, my friends have brought my lunch, and I need to eat and then have my nap." She leans her head back against her chair and closes her eyes.

I turn to the other ladies. "I'm Natalie Merin. I'm looking for my birth mother, Colleen Winters. She disappeared from here twenty years ago. Do either of you remember her?"

Marie shakes her head and glances at her friend. "No, sorry hon, we both moved here within the last ten years. But Alice has been here forever. She must've known her."

The other lady nods and bends down so her mouth is close to Alice's ear. "Do you remember her, Alice?"

Alice doesn't answer, and the woman yells louder. "Alice! Do you know what happened to..." She stops and looks at me. "What did you say her name is, hon?"

"Colleen Winters."

Alice starts at the sound of her name, but she keeps her eyes closed and shakes her head.

Why won't she talk about Colleen? What has changed

since I talked to her on the phone? Something has, and I need to find out what it is. Who didn't want me digging into Colleen's disappearance? Why didn't the people in town like her? "Alice, please tell me what happened to her. Who else in town knew my mother?"

Alice doesn't open her eyes or act like she knows I'm talking.

"Please."

Alice's eyes pop open and she points to the door. "Get out of here. Go home before it's too late."

The other ladies gasp.

"Too late for what?" I stare at the tiny old woman who stares back at me.

She sighs. "You don't understand the trouble you can cause by digging around in the past. Please, just go."

"I'll go if you answer one question for me."

Alice just looks at me.

"Is she still alive?"

Alice leans her head against the back of her chair. For a couple minutes I don't think she's going to answer. Then she says, "Dear God, I hope not."

CHAPTER 3: HELEN

Earlier that morning

We sit across the table from each other, two people whose history together is long and colorful. Bright blue mugs of hot coffee sit untouched, the steam rising in the air between us. It's early in the morning, and I've asked Jonas to meet me at the café, so we can talk. I drum my fingers on the table, a rat-a-tat-tat, that I know drives him crazy.

Jonas plays with a napkin, folding and refolding it. His silver hair brushes against the collar of his black polo shirt. For the first time this irritates me. "What do you think we should do?"

I stare at the table. Jonas doesn't seem surprised by what I've told him. "Alice said she's arriving today." I rub at the headache that's forming behind my eyes and hope it's not the beginning of a migraine. I've had more than my share and they always leave me feeling drained.

Jonas picks up his coffee cup. "How's Alice? I hear she's not doing well. Rumor has it that the diabetes is getting worse."

"Diabetes takes its toll on your body, even if you do your

best to take care of yourself, and we both know that Alice hasn't taken the best care of herself. She just quit drinking a couple years ago. That alone would cause problems, but she doesn't eat right, she's quit exercising, and her legs have just about given up on her."

Jonas shakes his head. "That's too bad." He takes a sip of coffee and sets the cup back down on the table. "That's hot. Now what did you say this girl's name is?"

"Natalie Merin." I watch him closely for any tell-tale sign that he knows who she is.

"Natalie Merin, why does that name ring a bell?"

"Leona Merin used to live here." I look into his eyes, searching for any recognition on his face.

"I don't remember a Leona. Must be someone else I've met over the years." He dismisses it with another head shake. "Alice says she's here looking for Colleen? Why would she come here looking for her after all these years?"

"Who knows what Colleen told her? She probably owes this girl money and told her she could get it from me." I rub at the knot in my left shoulder and take a deep breath, trying to force myself to relax, not wanting the migraine to catch hold of me.

Jonas stirs in his chair as though his back hurts. I give him a quick look, but his eyes are downcast, staring at the napkin as he begins to shred it. What's he thinking? Is he remembering what Colleen did to this town? What she did to me? I know I am. I've never forgotten the pain and embarrassment. I can feel it now in the burning nerve ends in my shoulders and up my neck. Colleen walked away, but I had to stay and keep the café open and endure all the gossip and disgust. I had to take care of our mother as she lay dying, crying for her baby girl.

"How many times did she disappear when she was young?"

"Well, you know she left when she was eighteen and was gone several years. Do you mean before that?"

"Yeah."

I sit back and dust the flour off my jeans, knowing I should get the bread started. Soon I'll have customers knocking on the door ready for breakfast. "She left when she was twelve, but Dad found her and brought her back. Then she left again when she was fifteen. She was gone several months that time. I thought Mom was going to starve herself to death worrying about her. I don't know if you remember, when she came home that time, she was so angry at my parents."

"Because they brought her home?"

"Yes. She claimed she could never live up to me. That Mom and Dad always compared her to me, and she came out on the bottom every time. But that wasn't true. Not of Mom, anyway. Who knows what Dad thought?"

I think about my father trying to survive in an alcoholic haze. He and Colleen had hated each other. Colleen wanted him to straighten up and quit drinking. She wanted him to be a real father to us, but he didn't have it in him, so she became him.

"He didn't know how to handle two teenage girls, especially Colleen. She was too challenging for him." I think of the fights they used to have and cringe. Mom and I would hide at the café, saying we had to work, but really, we just wanted away from the two of them. I was so happy to go away to college. Now I wonder if things would have turned out better if I'd stayed home and kept an eye on Colleen. "After she discovered her effect on boys, there was no stopping her."

"Colleen was a bad girl and loved to flaunt it."

Jonas smiles at some memory of Colleen's bad girl side, and I do the slow burn. How is it that after all this time my sister's affair with this man can still cause so much pain? I take a deep breath. I need to say what's on my mind. I've been holding it in for too many years. But he breaks in.

"Your mom had her hands full."

He doesn't mention that my dad spent most of his time in the bar telling everyone what a great woman he had while Mom worked herself into an early grave. After she died, he finally drank himself to death, which was a relief to me.

I look at Jonas, really look at him for the first time in years. I see the man I love has grown older. There are bags under his eyes and deep creases around his mouth. I grip my hands together. Even though we both married other people and tried to live our lives separately, it didn't work for either of us. It was temporary insanity on my part. After I married Douglas Bonner, Jonas jumped out and married Donna Ford. They were both hurt by us, an unnecessary pain we should have avoided. But I was tired of waiting for Jonas to man up and ask me to marry him. And now I know that I have left this conversation alone too long. "Jonas, I have to know something. What went on between you and Colleen?"

He looks up in surprise. "You aren't going to bring that up again, are you?"

I straighten my spine, tired of backing down, tired of letting him get away with things. It's time to face up to my shell of a life. "I have to, Jonas. I need to know what happened to Colleen. Was she pregnant and you paid her to leave town?" This is my deepest fear. I knew they had an affair, but the thought of Jonas having a child with her is more than I can bear. I wait silently for him to speak. I'm determined not to cry in front of him, but deep in my heart, I'm afraid this girl is his daughter, one he had with my sister, and I don't want the agony that truth will bring. Yet, today, I want to know the truth.

"You've got to be kidding me." He stands and towers over me. "What makes you think that? This girl coming to town? She's not my daughter, Helen. I have one child, Nick. Period. Okay?"

By now he's shouting and for a second, I think about backing down, trying to soothe him, a role I've played many times. But something inside of me won't let go. I've got to get him to admit that it's me he loves, that he still does, or we are finished. "How would I know, Jonas? You've never wanted to talk about it. We've gone all these years and not talked about it, and I'm tired of trying to second guess you." I stand up and face him, my arms wrapped tight around my waist, my mouth dry with fear. "Did you love her?"

"What the hell kind of question is that?" Jonas slams his chair against the table and coffee spills from both mugs. I watch it stream across the table and run onto the floor. Jonas storms out, slamming the door behind him.

Tears run down my face as I watch him go. We've had the same discussion over and over and it always ends this way. Why can't he tell me the truth? What's he hiding? I grab a rag and wipe up the coffee spill. As I do, I wonder who this girl is and why she has come to town. Why now? And why does her showing up here worry Jonas so much? I know why it worries me.

Present Day

My head spins as I walk down the road and turn right towards the center of town. When I asked Alice why she wanted Colleen to be dead, she screamed at me to leave. She became so agitated, her friend Marie followed me out onto the porch and said, "you'd better go. Maybe she'll calm down later and you can talk to her again."

The Sweet Onion Cafe sits between the laundry mat and a small grocery about a block from Alice's house. It once belonged to my mother's family. I found that out when I researched Cascade Locks before I left Florida. A woman I met at dinner last night told me that it belongs to Helen Bonner. I wonder if she bought it from the Winters, or if she's related to them. Maybe she's related to me.

When I open the door, I'm hit with the rich fragrance of coffee and the warm sweet smell of cinnamon rolls. I step inside and hope I'll find someone here who knew Colleen.

According to my online search, there are no Winters in Cascade Locks now. It's like the family moved or died out. I'm sure that Alice knows, but I don't know why she won't tell me. I saw the fear on her face and in her voice. It was so heavy in that house. What's she so afraid of? I wonder. Icy fingers tickle my skin. A premonition? I hope not.

The first person I see when I enter the café is a man about my age. He's sitting by himself, looking at me and smiling. Is everyone in this town so friendly? It's weird to me because in Kissimmee, the city where I'm from in Florida, no one smiles at you unless they know you. I give him a tentative smile and walk to the back to order coffee and a cinnamon roll.

The girl behind the counter's name tag reads, Lindsey. She looks like some of the girls in my English classes at home, with her long brown hair and short cutoffs. Her boots are black and come to her knee. I can't help but notice that teen fashions are the same out west as they are in the east. Lindsey has a big smile on her face as she asks for my order. "Just passing through or staying in town for a while?"

I'm not used to people asking my intentions and she catches me off-guard. "I..um...I'm actually staying in town for a few days."

"Cool. There's so much to see and do here. Do you like to hike? We have hiking trails and the most beautiful waterfalls." She puts a hand to her chest like she's describing her first crush. "They're so gorgeous. You should make sure you see some of them while you're here."

I nod and hand her the money she asks for, feeling a little unnerved by her friendliness. She gives me change and some of it drops from my hand to the floor. The man who smiled at me when I first came in is standing next to me, money in his hand to pay his bill. He leans down and picks it up and hands it to me. Our fingers brush and I feel his touch down to my toes. I pull back and stare at him. My first thought is, wow! He's gorgeous! He's tall and has dark brown hair that curls over his forehead. His eyes are a deep brown and warm as the earth with the sun shining on it. Hannah would say, yummy. I try not to smile as I think of her response to the handsome man in front of me.

"Ooooh, you should totally hike up the trail at Mult-nomah Falls. It's our most famous falls. It's huge and you can walk to the top," Lindsey says as she hands me the latte I asked for.

I drag my eyes away from the man next to me and turn towards her. I don't remember saying I liked to hike, but I do, so I smile and say, "Okay, thanks. I'll have to try it."

"There are many hiking trails around," the guy standing next to me says. His voice is deep and soft, like the rumble of thunder in the distance, it plays over my skin causing me to shiver. "Enjoy your stay."

He turns and walks away, and I follow him with my eyes. When I turn back around, Lindsey is giving me a knowing look. "Cute butt, huh?"

She surprises a laugh out of me, and I almost spew coffee across the floor.

A slender woman with long white hair pulled back into a ponytail walks around the counter and hands me a cinnamon roll as big as the blue plate it's sitting on. I feel my eyes widen at its size and look up to thank her. For the first time since I've arrived in town, I meet an unfriendly face. She gives me a look like I was formed from the grime under her feet and walks away.

I stare at her wondering why she's being so rude? I'm not used to being looked at like I'm scum. I start to say something to Lindsey, but she's helping another customer, so I sit down and drink my coffee and try to eat a bite of the cinnamon roll that now tastes like sawdust. Why did the woman look at me like that? Is she the owner, Helen

Bonner? Is she in love with the cute guy and doesn't want any competition? She's old enough to be his mother!

I sit for a while, drinking my coffee and thinking about how creeped out I was with the friendly people. Now I'm creeped out by this woman who acts like I'm Satan's daughter. I try to brush off the feeling. As I take tiny bites of my dessert, I feel stabs of darts in my back. Then the feeling eases and I look up and see her disappearing into another room.

Lindsey comes over to see how I'm doing, and I motion her closer. "Who's the woman who was working behind the counter?"

"Helen? She's the owner."

"Do you know anyone in town with the last name Winters?" I pop another bite of cinnamon roll in my mouth and chew it slowly, even though the pleasure in the warm sweetness is gone.

Lindsey stands next to me, her finger on her lips, thinking. "No, I don't think so. I know most of the people in town, but that name doesn't ring a bell."

"I was told this café belonged to the Winters' family at one time.

"Hmm, I don't know. You can ask Helen. She'll probably know."

Lindsey moves back to make an espresso for another customer, her boots clomping against the wood floor, and I sit starring at my blue cup. So, the woman who gave me a look like she'd like to see me dead, owns this place. I hate the thought of striking up a conversation with her, but she might know the Winters. She might even know my mother. I try to think of a way to bring up the previous owners, but she sees me looking at her and turns and heads out the back door.

I stand up and take tip money from my bag and practically throw it at Lindsey. Then I hurry to the back door of the café and step out, looking around for Helen Bonner. She's standing, leaning against a shed, a cigarette in her hand.

"Helen?"

She turns her icy blue eyes on me. "This area is for employees only."

"I just want to talk to you for a minute." I stand in front of her feeling like I've been sent to the principal's office. I take the picture of Colleen out of my bag and hold it up for her to see.

She looks away, but not before recognition flashes in her eyes. She knows the woman in the picture.

Helen takes a puff of her cigarette. She doesn't say anything, so I burst into conversation, my voice high and squeaky. "I'm looking for a woman who used to live here... Colleen Winters." I shove the photo under her nose. "She lived here about twenty years ago. Is this her? Do you know her?"

Helen bends over and puts out her cigarette in a potted plant. Then she straightens up and looks me in the eye. "Not anymore."

"Did she move away?"

Helen shrugs. "Must have. She hasn't been around for a long time."

"Are you related to her?" I'm starting to feel depressed, realizing that this woman has no intention of telling me what I want to know.

"Who I'm related to or not is none of your business. Now if you'll excuse me, I have to get back to work." She walks around me back into the café. As I watch, she disappears out a door on the other side.

I run after her. "Helen, I just want to talk to you." She ignores me and walks into a building that looks like an old garage. I run up and try the door, but it's locked.

"Well, that was helpful." I whisper to myself as I go back into the café and out the front door. Lindsey calls a cheerful, "come see us again," as I pass her. *Oh, I will, have no doubt about that.*

Outside I make my way slowly down the street towards the hotel. I have a lot to think about. There's a tour bus sitting in the hotel parking lot and people are everywhere, up and down the sidewalk, heading for the river and the ice cream place across the street. A woman bumps into me, and I try to move out of her way, but to my surprise she grabs my arm. "I need to talk to you."

Alarmed, I try and pull away, but she has a firm grasp on my arm. "Who are you?"

"Just keep walking. We'll talk in private."

Her voice is low and rough, and it frightens me. I stop in my tracks and tear my arm from her tight hold. "No, you tell me right now what you want or I'm not going a step further."

People move around us on the sidewalk, giving us funny looks. The woman reaches for me again, but I move away. She comes closer. "Believe me, you want to hear what I have to say. It's about your mother."

"My mother? How do you know my mother?"

"I don't really, but I've heard about her. If you want to know what I know, follow me." She lets go of my arm and after a half a second, I follow her.

We cross the street and find a bench outside my hotel. The woman sits down and pats the space next to her. "I heard you asking about the Winters' family in the café, so I looked at you and it hit me, you're the image of Colleen Winters."

My heart skips a beat. *Finally, someone who admits knowing Colleen.* I turn towards her, sitting close, leaning towards her like we are old friends who haven't seen each other in ages. "You knew her? Do you know what happened to her?"

The woman, who tells me her name is Gayle Woods, nods, and leans closer. "The story is that she ran off in 1996 and never returned."

"Did anyone look for her? I asked Alice Perkins and she said everyone in town despised Colleen, but she wouldn't tell me why. Do you know why?"

Gayle shakes her head. She's a small woman who once was probably a beauty. She has platinum blonde hair, and her skin looks weathered from too many trips to the tanning booth. "No, but I do know she had a huge fight with her sister the night she disappeared. Huge. They really hated each other. And then no one ever saw her again."

"Sister?"

Gayle's eyes grow large behind her white designer glasses. "You don't know, do you?"

"Know what?"

She points towards the café. "Helen is Colleen's sister."

Suddenly things begin to make sense, like why Helen acted the way she did. She must know that I'm Colleen's daughter. "She didn't want to talk about Colleen."

"I heard they fought like crazy. Helen hated her sister."

"Do you know why?" If Helen fought with her sister just before she left town, she probably feels guilty about Colleen's disappearance. Maybe that's why she doesn't want to talk to me.

"Probably because of Jonas. Helen has been in love with him since she was a teenager. And Colleen wanted him."

"Who's Jonas?"

"Jonas White. His family was one of the first to settle in this town way back when. Jonas owns most of the land around here. He has a construction company that builds high end houses in the gorge." She waves her arm around, her face becoming animated. "If you get out and drive around, you can't help but notice them on the cliffs over-looking the river. He and his son, Nick, are partners and the houses they build are amazing. Jonas is..." she stops talking and laughs a light tinkling sound. "Jonas is gorgeous. He's movie star handsome and so is Nick, of course."

I notice the blush on her face and realize she has a huge crush on Jonas White. "So, you think Helen and Colleen fought over Jonas?"

"Yes, and I'm pretty sure it didn't end well for Colleen." She tries to look concerned, but it doesn't show in her eyes. She's too eager to tell me about Colleen and Helen's fight.

Shivers like pings of ice on a snowy day scatter over my skin. I grab the end of the bench and hold on, my nails sinking into the wood. "What do you think happened to her?"

Gayle shrugs. She lowers her voice. "You figure it out. They had a big fight and Colleen was never seen again."

I put my hand over my mouth, holding in the gasp, feeling my eyes grow wide. "You think Helen killed her?"

"I think someone did, and Helen had more reason than anyone else to want her dead." Gayle stands and smiles down at me.

"Did you know my mother?" I stand up next to her.

Gayle shakes her head. "Not really. I saw her around, but I didn't know her."

"Can you prove that she's dead? That someone killed her?"

"No, it's up to you to prove whether she is or not. I just thought that since you're looking for Colleen, you should look closely at Helen."

As she turns to walk away, I wonder what Colleen did to make people here dislike her so much.

CHAPTER 5: NATALIE

Present Day

I run after Gayle, calling her name. My heart aches for the mother I never knew. Maybe Gayle's wrong and Colleen left because of the fight. Just because she and Helen fought doesn't mean she's dead, does it? Why does Gayle want Helen to be a murderer? I wish I could make Helen talk to me.

"Wait! You think Helen would kill her sister because she stole her boyfriend?"

Gayle stops and looks down at me from her position at the top of the stairs leading to the parking lot. "No, not just because of that. Colleen made her family the laughing-stock of Cascade Locks."

"How?"

"For some reason, Colleen was determined to sleep with every guy in town who would sleep with her and give her drugs and booze, including Jonas and the Mayor and... the list is long and includes most of the prominent families of this town.

"The women of Cascade Locks hated her and wanted

her to leave. Helen was looked down on because she was her sister." She looks at her watch. "I've got to go. Think about what I said and be careful who you talk to about this. This town has deep-seated ideas about Colleen Winters. She's almost a legend."

"It's been twenty years. You'd think they would be over it by now."

Gayle shrugs. "You'd think so, but all I've ever heard was that no one wanted to talk about her. She did something horrible, even worse than sleeping with every man she could, but I don't know what it was."

After she leaves, I think about everything I've learned. There's something that Helen and Alice don't want me to find out. Did Helen kill my mother like Gayle thinks, or is she covering up for Alice? Or is Alice covering up for her? How am I going to find out if no one but Gayle will talk to me?

I get up and head back to my room, my thoughts all jumbled. The two women I need answers from won't talk to me, maybe I should find a different source. I pick up my iPhone and google an address for White Construction, Jonas White's business. I find it and from the map of Cascade Locks I picked up I see it's on the outskirt of town, so I head to my car. I want to see the man who had my mother and her sister fighting over him. He must be something.

The red Mustang I rented sits in the parking lot where I left it when I first got to town. I get in and head east. The Construction Company is located on WaNaPa Street, just passed the edge of town. I pull up and get out. The building is large and creamed colored with an office attached. There's a full-size white pick-up with White Construction written on the side sitting next to the office door and I breathe a sigh of relief that Jonas White is there.

When I open the door, a young woman with coal black hair wearing blue framed glasses and red lipstick looks up. "Hi, what can I do for you?"

"I'm looking for Jonas White. Is he in?"

She shakes her head. "No, sorry. He just called and said he's headed to Portland. Nick's in, though. Want me to buzz him?"

"Nick?"

A door opens behind me and I turn to look and the great looking guy from the café steps out. My nerve ends tingle. "Jenna, can you call..." he stops talking when he sees me. "Hi, didn't I just see you at the café?" He turns the full force of his sexy smile on me and it takes my breath away.

I smile and hold out my hand. "I'm Natalie Marin."

He shakes my hand. "Nick White. What can I do for you?"

"I'm actually looking for Jonas."

"Dad's gone to Portland for supplies. Were you looking for a contractor?"

I study him. He's too young to have known my birth mother, but he may know something. He smiles and I feel a small dip in my stomach. He smells of the outdoors and something a little sweet and spicy. He's good-looking in a GQ way. I'm used to the guys I teach high school with who dress more casually. Nick White is a businessman who looks like he knows his position in life and likes it. If his father looks anything like him, I'm not surprised my mother and Helen fought over him.

"It's personal."

He looks startled but invites me back to his office.

"Come on back and we'll talk." He hands Jenna a file and leads the way to a door next to a small hallway.

His office is tastefully and expensively decorated, with a dark cherry wood desk and a burgundy leather chair. There are bookcases on one wall filled with design books and two chairs that match the desk chair. He motions me into one of them and takes his place behind the desk.

"Is there something I can do for you?" His warm blue eyes seduce me. I want to melt into them. I don't remember when, if ever, a guy has had this effect on me.

I blink and sit up straight, pushing that thought away. I'm here for a reason and good-looking men are not what I'm looking for right now. "I'm searching for Colleen Winters. I was told your father knows her." I find myself not wanting to believe Alice or Gayle. I still hope that Colleen's alive.

Nick frowns and leans back in his chair. "Helen's sister," he says, slowly. "I haven't thought of her in years. She left town when I was a kid and never returned. Did you ask Helen about her?"

I cross my legs and try to relax. Since talking to Gayle, I've felt wound so tight I may come undone any second. I take a deep breath. "Yes, but she wouldn't talk to me."

Nick's eyes widen. "Interesting. She's probably embarrassed."

"Why?"

He looks at the ceiling and I can tell he's thinking about what to say. "Rumor is that Colleen did something that upset people in this town. That was way back before either of us were born. I've never heard all the details, but I hear it was bad."

"Was she accused of a crime?" My heart thuds with dread.

"Not that I know of, but like I said, I was really young when she left. Dad could probably tell you more if he was here. Why don't you leave a phone number and I'll have him call you?"

My heart sinks. I was hoping Jonas would be here and tell me where Colleen was. I give Nick my cell number. "Please tell him it's important," I say as I stand to go.

Nick accompanies me to the door. "I will. By the way, why are you looking for Colleen?"

I give him a sad smile and say, "I'm pretty sure she's my birth mother."

"Oh crap. I'm so sorry. I shouldn't have said anything."

I'm about to tell him it's okay when the outer door opens and an older version of Nick walks in. His hair has a little silver at the temples and his eyes aren't the rich sky blue of his son's. He's not as tall or as lean as Nick, but you can tell they're related.

"Forgot to pick up the check for that..." He stops dead when he sees me, and his face turns white. We stare at each other for a couple minutes and then he grabs the check Jenna placed on the counter in front of him and heads for the door. "Sorry, I've got to go."

I run after him. "Mr. White, Jonas. Please, I need to talk to you."

He stops and turns to me. "Sorry, I've got to get to Portland." He doesn't look sorry as he jumps in his pickup and drives away.

Nick follows me outside and there's silence between us as we watch his father's white pickup, a twin to the one sitting in the driveway, which I assume is Nick's, disappear around a corner. "He was in a hurry."

"Yes." Nick scratches his head. "He must be late for an appointment."

Jenna comes to the door and yells, "Nick, Mr. Sanders is on the phone. Says it's important."

"Okay, I'll be right there." He turns to me. "I'll talk to my dad when he gets back. Maybe I can get him to open up about Colleen."

I nod and head to my car. "Thank you." I hear the gravel crunch under my sandals, the sounds of sea gulls squawking overhead, feel the heat of the sun, but inside I'm ice cold.

"I'll be in touch." Nick lifts a hand in farewell as he heads back into the office.

As I drive back to my hotel, which takes all of five minutes, I think about what to do next. How can I make people here talk to me about Colleen? I'm so tired of lies and deception. I've had a lifetime of being lied to, even though I didn't know it at the time. Why would Leona adopt me, tell me that she's my grandmother, and lie about my real mother? None of it makes sense and I'm devastated by the weight of her lies. I also miss Leona like crazy, which really makes me angry at myself. I touch my chest where there's a knife-edged pain. We were so close until she passed, and I found out she'd lied to me my entire life.

At the hotel, I use my key card to get into my room. The curtains are open, and the serene beauty of the river calls to me. I walk inside and step on a piece of paper. Wondering where it came from, I bend down and pick it up. Written in block letters with black ink are the words:

STOP ASKING QUESTIONS. GO HOME BEFORE IT'S TOO LATE.

CHAPTER 6: NICK

Present Day

After I take care of the phone call, I look out the window and watch Natalie walk away from our office building to her car. Her blonde ponytail swings with each step she takes, and I can't take my eyes off of her. She gets in her car and drives out of sight.

My father's reaction to Natalie's questions surprises me. What's he trying to hide? My dad has never been known for being subtle, but today he was outright rude to a beautiful woman and that's something else Jonas never does.

What did Colleen Winters do to this town? I've heard stories over the years, but Dad never wanted to talk about her. Natalie seems determined to find her, and I hope that she's everything Natalie wants her to be.

I clean my desk, doing busy work to keep my mind away from Natalie. Sure, she's beautiful, but it sounds like she has a lot of baggage and the last thing I need is a woman with baggage. I had more of that than I could handle with Danny's mother. I loved Liz, but she was wounded emotionally before she found out about the cancer.

Why am I always drawn to women who need something? Why can't I find a woman who has everyday problems, like what to have for dinner and where to find a job? Oh no, not me. I find the ones who are broken and need more than I can give them.

I promised Natalie I'd ask Jonas about Colleen, so I pick up my cell phone and dial my dad's number. Jonas answers right away, but his voice is cautious. "What's up?"

"Where are you? Did you get to Portland?"

"I'm on my way. Did you get rid of that nosey woman?"

"Do you mean Natalie? She thinks Colleen Winters is her birth mother. Do you know what happened to her?"

There's silence on the other end of the phone for a few minutes. "No, and from what I remember about Colleen Winters, Natalie is better off not finding her. She wasn't great mother material."

"Then just tell Natalie that. You were rude to her today." I paced my office.

"I was not. She caught me off guard. I haven't thought about Colleen in years."

"What did she do? Natalie says no one wants to talk to her about Colleen, even Helen. Especially Helen. Why won't she talk to Natalie? That seems strange and not like her. What would it hurt to tell the girl about her birth mother?"

Jonas sighs, a deep rusty sound that annoys me more than usual. I can see him rolling his eyes. "Drop it, Nick. You don't want to go there, believe me."

"Why? What did she do that was so terrible?"

Dad is silent, and I take a deep breath and let it out slowly. "I get it you don't want to talk about her, Dad. But if I'm any judge of character, I'd say Natalie is going to keep looking for Colleen until she finds out where she is."

"You might want to tell her to stop. If you like her that is, and it sure sounds like you're interested. Listen son, Colleen wasn't a good person. She caused destruction everywhere she went, and she'll cause heartache for Natalie, too. Tell her to go back to Florida. Save herself some agony."

"I can't do that."

"Can't or won't? She's a beautiful girl, Nick. But if you have any brains about you, stay away from her. If she's anything like her mother, she's not worth pursuing."

Jonas hangs up before I can comment. I feel my jaws ache from clenching them so hard. Why couldn't Jonas just tell me what Colleen did that was so bad? Maybe I should talk to Helen.

I decide to call it a day. I know in my gut that I should stay away from Natalie; that trying to help her would only bring more trouble.

Why do I feel the need to help, anyway? Maybe I should just forget about her. Why should I get involved in her problems? Then I think about the sad look in her beautiful blue eyes and the sweet but determined set to her chin. *Well, hell.*

CHAPTER 7: HELEN

Present Day

I barely make it in my front door before the blinding pain in my head forces me to my knees. I hold my hands against my skull and try to stand long enough to walk into the kitchen for the pain pills the doctor prescribed. I down two with a glass of water, hoping they'll stay down this time.

Fumbling my way into the bedroom, I kick off my shoes and curl up on the bed, hoping the pills will take affect before my head bursts all over the down comforter and the walls of my room. In my mind, I can see my brains spread around in bright colors of purple, red and yellow. *Please make the pain stop,* I pray, holding my head and lying back against the comforter.

The moment Natalie walked into the café I saw Colleen as she looked twenty-five years ago. Long before the alcohol and the hard life toughened her features, Colleen had the same soft porcelain skin, soft blue eyes and turned up nose. Her hair had been short and straight instead of the long curls that Natalie wears, but the resemblance is uncanny. I can't get my head around the fact that Colleen has a daughter. *I have a niece.*

I push against my temples, not wanting to think about my sister. I've had twenty years of peace. It hasn't been a perfect twenty years. I've had a lot of bad things in my life, but after my childhood and all the problems with Colleen, the last few years have been pure bliss.

Images of the last time I saw my sister force themselves into my mind even though I try hard to think about something else; the smell of bread baking, the first cup of coffee in the morning, the taste of a cigarette after quitting for the zillionth time. But nothing keeps the thoughts of that night from bombarding my mind.

There are so many what-ifs I think as I hold my head and rock back and forth on the bed. What if that boy hadn't died? What if Jonas hadn't cheated on me with my sister? What if I'd been able to forgive him? Of course, Colleen wouldn't let that happen. She'd had to brag about sleeping with Jonas, like she bragged about every guy she slept with. Most of them were probably lies, she told so many lies.

The phone on the end table by my bed peals, and I groan and hold on tighter to my head. *Leave me alone. Please God, make them leave me alone.* I hear my employee, Lindsey's voice, "Helen, are you home? Where are you? I'm worried. Call me when you get this."

After a few minutes of writhing on the bed, the pain eases a tiny bit and I feel myself begin to relax. Soon the blessed sleep will come, and I won't have to think about anything. Not the café, not Jonas and especially not my sister.

It's so stupid of me to try and make Jonas say he loves me. I'm so pathetic, but I desperately want to hear that it has always been me that he loves. I know I should've kept my mouth shut that morning, but I need to know how he feels about me. I'm so tired of pretending that things are good between us. I know I've become a convenience to Jonas, someone to have sex with, but not to have a life with. What if Colleen hadn't been around back then? Would things have turned out better? What if she comes back now?

My temple throbs and I rub my forehead and try and get comfortable. I can smell Jonas' scent on my pillow, and I think about the last time he was here with me. How wonderful it was to feel his body against me, inside me, warm and strong and eager. And how bereft I felt when he left early the next morning, saying he had to go home before he could go to work.

I want to stay in the dream where Jonas loves me. Where he's willing to stay with me all night, cuddled under the down comforter. And he's still here the next morning, reading the newspaper while I fix breakfast---the dream where his ring is on my finger and his clothes in my closet.

Colleen has been gone for twenty years. Why would she come back now? Unless she needs money? She always tried her best to get money out of me. When I put my foot down and told her I absolutely would not invest any more of my hard-earned money into one of her get-rich schemes, Colleen went to Jonas. She knew if she could get to Jonas it would hurt me more than anything.

I lean into the pillow, thinking about the night Colleen left. We'd had a horrible fight after we closed the café. Colleen acted like she had a juicy secret all evening. She smirked as she passed me while delivering food to our customers. She'd talked and laughed and flirted with every guy who walked through the door, which wasn't unusual. I ignored her, going about my business.

Finally, everyone, including our cook, Alice Perkins,

left. We were cleaning, and Colleen started talking about Jonas. She knew I had been in love with Jonas since high school.

Finally, I'd had enough and confronted my sister. "What are you trying to say, Colleen? You've been making snide remarks and comments about Jonas all night. What are you getting at?"

Colleen grinned and shrugged her shoulders. "I don't know what you mean. I'm just talking."

"Fine." I went back to work, but of course Colleen couldn't let it go.

"We've got to hurry. Jonas is picking me up in a half hour. We're going to that new place in Portland everyone's talking about."

"Excuse me? You and Jonas are going out tonight?" I stood next to her my hands clenched at my side. Jonas and I were practically engaged, and she knew it. We had a date the next night and I was sure he planned to put a ring on my finger.

Colleen looked at her fingernails. "I should have worn the dark red polish."

I grabbed her arm. "I asked you a question."

Colleen smiled, her eyes dancing. "That's right. He's taking me to Portland. We'll probably spend the night." She laughed and headed towards the closet where we kept our cleaning supplies. "I wouldn't wait up."

"You bitch!" I cried, grabbing her arm, and spinning her around. "You know Jonas and I are dating again. And even if we weren't, how could you spend the night with him?"

Colleen tried to shrug me off. "It's easy, really, we've been doing it for weeks."

I threw myself on my sister, pulling her hair and punching her. It was as though I was inside a black cloud and couldn't feel anything except anger. Colleen fought back like a wild cat. We'd always fought like this, going for each other like two crazy people, but this night was different. This time it was much more intense. I'd had enough and wanted to beat the smugness out of her.

How we wound up outside, I can never remember. But I remember the cool night air, the darkness, and the sound of our breathing, quick and fast in the night. I remember the grunts, the name calling, the screams, and then Colleen got away, grabbed something and the next thing I felt was excruciating pain in the side of my head and blessed darkness.

CHAPTER 8: COLLEEN

Thirty years ago

I hurried home, snuck into the house, grabbed my coat and another flashlight, and headed to Jose's, hoping those creeps had lied to me.

What I really wanted was to stay home and take a long hot shower. I felt so dirty where that creep touched me. I scrubbed at my thighs with my hands as I walked knowing I'd have to throw my dress away as soon as I took it off. Where was Jose? What if they'd beat him up and left him bleeding? He might need a doctor.

Jose lived with his parents in a small single-wide trailer on Ruckle Street. It wasn't far from our house on Tahoma. I hurried in that direction, taking the back way and hiding every time I thought I heard someone coming.

There were no lights on in Jose's house when I got there. His dad's truck was parked in the drive, along with an old white Ford SUV that belonged to his mother. I crept up to the car and peeked inside, my heart thudding because I was afraid of what I might find.

I turned on my flashlight and shone it inside the car. I

didn't see anything. Where was Jose? Did Larry and Steve lie to me, trying to get me to go with them? I shuddered at the thought of what I'd escaped.

Since I didn't see anything and the lights were off in his house, I assumed Jose was inside asleep. I breathed a sigh of relief and headed back home.

I hadn't gone far when I heard a car coming my way. I hid behind a tree and watched as it pulled slowly up the street and stopped at Jose's house. That's when I realized it was a Sheriff's car, and I felt tears spurt from my eyes.

"Oh, no, dear God, no," I cried silently as the door opened and two officers climbed out and made their way to Jose's door.

I stood with my hand over my mouth, my heart pounding, and watched as a light came on and Mr. Santiago came to the door. I couldn't hear what the police said to him, but he crumpled to the ground, and I heard his cries in the night. In that moment, I knew what had happened as surely as if I was standing next to them. Jose was dead, and I knew who killed him.

I didn't feel my feet touch the ground as I flew through the night to the Sheriff's side. I threw myself at him and he caught me. "Please," I said between gasps of breath, "is it Jose? Is he okay?"

The Sheriff shook his head. Everardo came out of the house and took his father in his arms. Mr. Santiago cried out, his chest heaving. Tears dripped down Everardo's face.

The deputy took me from the sheriff's arms. "Who are you?" he asked me gently.

I told him my name. "I'm Jose's friend. We were supposed to meet tonight, but he didn't show up."

"Please tell me what happened," Everardo said, gritting

his teeth, trying to be brave. "What happened to my brother?"

"I'm sorry." The sheriff shook his head. "Mr. Santiago, your son was found by the old Zohler place. He was beat up bad."

"Is he alive?" Everardo asked.

The sheriff looked at Everardo and again gave his head a shake. "I'm so sorry. There was nothing we could do."

Mr. Santiago cried out in Spanish and Everardo said, "My father wants to know where you've taken him."

"We called an ambulance to take him to the hospital in Hood River."

Every word he said was like a branding iron on my soul. I tasted hate, as bitter as the black mud that lay close to the river. "I can tell you who did it," I said, and they all looked at me. "Larry White and Steve Perkins beat him up and left him to die. Then they attacked me."

The deputy shone his flashlight on me. He saw my torn dress, which I tried to hold together with my hands so my underwear wouldn't show and blood from the cuts on my knees and elbows. "They raped you?"

I started to tell them that no, they were stopped before they could, but they tried. But for some reason the words wouldn't come out and I burst into tears. I heard the deputy call in a murder and a rape. I heard Mr. Santiago and Everardo wailing as I slipped from the officer's arms to the ground in a dead faint.

CHAPTER 9: NATALIE

Present Day

I bend down and pick up the paper from off the floor. My hands are shaking, and the paper slips, but I grab it before it falls. My first thought when I look at what is written, is that Alice left it there. But how would she get the note under my door? It doesn't look like she can move very far. What about Helen? I know she doesn't want me here. She doesn't want me asking questions about Colleen. It must be Helen. *How dare she!*

Anger builds in me like a volcano about to burst through the earth. I grab my phone, find the number for the Sweet Onion Café and with trembling fingers, touch the numbers to make the call. A voice I recognize as Lindsey's answers right away.

"I want to speak to Helen."

"I'm sorry...um...Helen's not here right now. Can I give her a message?"

I hear the frustration in Lindsey's voice and raised voices in the background. "Do you know where she is?"

"No, but I'm sure she'll be right back. I'm sorry, I have

to go. If you want to leave a message for Helen, I'll give it to her."

"No, that's okay." Without giving my name, I end the call. I'm gritting my teeth so tight, my jaw aches. How dare that woman try to run me out of town?

Deciding I need to walk off my anger, I grab my bag, throw my phone in it, grab my keycard and head for the river. Maybe a walk will calm me.

There's a path from the hotel to the river. I follow it and notice people walking, riding bikes and scooters along a paved path that runs alongside the water. The Bridge of the Gods is close to the hotel and I watch as cars travel back and forth between Oregon and Washington. I can hear the singing of their tires on the metal bridge. It looms overhead like a spaceship hovering over the earth.

As I walk, I feel myself begin to calm down. Nick said Helen Bonner is a nice person. That means I---or more likely Colleen---bring out the worst in her. *What did you do?* I silently ask Colleen.

My cellphone rings and I see my best friend's name pop up. Hannah Laurence and I have been friends since middle school. We're both teachers now, but Hannah is taking maternity leave. Her first baby is due any minute.

"Hey girl, do we have a baby yet?"

She sighs over the phone. "I wish. This kid has her own timetable. I just got back from the doctor and he said it won't be long now. When are you coming home?"

I feel the anger inside me begin to ebb. Just hearing Hannah's voice brings me back from the anger bursting inside of me. "I just got here." So much has happened already that it feels like I've been in Oregon much longer than I have. "I'm not sure how long this will take."

"Tell me everything. I'm living vicariously through you now."

I tell her what all I've found out about my birth mother since arriving, ending with how Helen left the threatening note in my room.

"I don't like that, Natalie. She sounds unbalanced. Maybe you should stay away from her."

I stop and watch as a little red-haired boy throws rocks into the river. One makes a big splash and he laughs and leaning down grabs another. "She may be the only one here who knows what happened to my mother. I need her to tell me what she knows."

"How about Alice? You said she's old. Maybe she'll feel more like talking tomorrow."

"I hope so." We visit a while, and I watch the redheaded boy lean out to throw another rock. He looks about six-years-old but could be younger. As he tosses the rock his feet slip, and he almost tumbles down the cliff into the water. My heart does flip flops as I run to him. My cellphone falls to the ground as I reach out and grab the back of his shirt to pull him back. His feet dangle over the side for a minute before I'm able to get hold of him with both hands and we slide to the ground in a heap, his tiny body on top of mine.

He gives me a big grin, but I can hear his heart thudding inside his little chest. "Thanks, that was close."

"It sure was." I hold him to me for a second, letting our heartbeats settle down. Then I fumble for my cellphone and hold it up to my ear. "Hannah, I've got to go. I'll call you when I know more, okay? And let me know when my goddaughter arrives."

"You'll probably hear me scream with relief from Florida," she says. We say goodbye and hang up.

I look down at the boy who is now trying to pry a stick loose from its attachment to the ground. "Where's your mom?"

He shakes his head. "I don't have a mom. She died. I'm living with my dad."

I want to sink into the ground with sympathy. Another displaced child. "I'm sorry." The words come out soft and rubbery.

He grins up at me. "Don't be sorry. She died when I was little, and I have the best dad in the world. He takes care of me."

"Does he know that you're out here by yourself? You could've fallen in the river if I hadn't been close."

"Don't tell him, okay?"

He has no concept that I don't have a clue who his father is.

"Chloe is supposed to be watching me, but her boyfriend came along, and they want to be alone, so they can kiss each other." He makes a gagging motion.

"She left you here to go off with her boyfriend?"

"Nah, she's over there." He points to a couple on the lawn by the hotel.

They are so far away that Chloe couldn't have gotten to him in time if he'd tumbled into the water. Besides, she isn't hurrying over, so I assume she wasn't watching him very closely. The teacher in me wants to march over and tell her what I think of her not paying attention to her charge, but she and her boyfriend are so involved in each other that I decide it probably won't do any good.

"I think you need a different babysitter." I mutter under my breath.

"What's your name?" he asks, "mine's Danny." He holds out his hand and shakes mine.

"Hi, Danny. I'm Natalie." I smile at his good manners.

"Hey Dad, over here," Danny yells and I watch as Nick White jogs up the path to join us.

Nick stops next to us and gives me one of his killer smiles. It's a good thing I won't be around Cascade Locks long, I decide as I look into his goregeous eyes. The man does something to me.

Danny's babysitter, the girl named, Chloe, comes over. Her face is red, and she has grass in her hair. She's pulling down her top and making sure her shorts are snapped. "Nick, I didn't think you were going to be here for another half hour."

Nick looks from her to the teenage boy who is heading in the opposite direction. There's no softening of understanding on his face and I feel a tiny bit sorry for Chloe. "Obviously. I thought we talked about you inviting your boyfriend to spend time with you when you're looking out for Danny."

"Yeah, I almost fell in the river and Natalie had to save me. You were too busy kissing on your boyfriend. Yuck."

Nick looks from Danny to me, one eyebrow raised in question. "He was close to the edge."

"Yeah, real close. I thought I was a goner. But Natalie grabbed my shirt." Danny's eyes sparkle with excitement and I realize he's not at all traumatized by his almost fall.

"I'm sorry," Chloe says, brushing her long hair away from her face. "It won't happen again. I thought Trevor only had time to stop for a second, but he had more time and we got to talking and...it won't happen again."

"No, it won't." Nick takes his wallet out and gives her some money. "I have to be able to trust you, Chloe. What if Danny had fallen in the river? It's so swift; we may have never found him again." Nick's face is white, and Chloe's is a deep red.

"I'm sorry," she says again. Then she stuffs the money into her bag and takes off. I see tears in her eyes as she leaves, but I can't summon up much sympathy. Danny could've died.

"Did I say thank-you?" Nick asks, his voice deep with concern.

I shake my head. "It's not needed. I'm glad I was here." I turn to Danny. "It was so nice to meet you, Danny. Try and stay away from the edge from now on, okay?"

Danny grins, his freckles standing out on his pale face. He has a grin that could melt the hardest heart. Mine, of course, isn't that hard.

"Dad and I are going to get a burger at the Bridgeside restaurant. Want to join us? She can, can't she Dad?" He looks up at his father with a hopeful look on his face.

Apparently, Nick doesn't know what to say at first because he doesn't say anything for longer than is comfortable. "No, that's okay." I wave my hand and start to turn away.

"Wait. You gotta eat. Come on, Dad, tell Natalie we want her to have lunch with us." He squints up at his dad.

"Yes, of course. Join us."

I'm starving, but I don't want to butt in on their lunch. I start to say no, but when I look at Danny's hopeful face, I give in. How can I tell him no? Besides, I want to ask Nick about Helen. I don't know what to do. Nick doesn't seem all that excited to have company, but I agree anyway. "That will be great."

Danny whoops and runs ahead of us to the restaurant that's next to my hotel. "Is he always this exuberant?" I ask Nick.

Nick laughs, and I can feel him relax. "Always. He's a typical redheaded six-year-old. He has so much energy that it's everything I can do to keep up with him." He's smiling, but a dark look washes over his face. "I can't imagine what would have happened if you hadn't been there and reacted so quickly."

"I'm glad I was. He's a great little boy."

We make our way into the restaurant. It's a Monday afternoon in July and the small town is full. I look around and think all the tourists must be there to eat, the place is packed. "We may not get a table," I say to Nick.

He turns his head and smiles. "I know the owner."

From out of the back comes a middle-aged woman wearing black slacks and a white blouse. Her blonde hair is pulled up into a clip and she wears black framed glasses that sit on the end of her nose. She kisses Nick on the cheek and ruffles Danny's hair. "How are my boys today? Need a table? We can seat you out on the deck if you'd like."

I'm embarrassed when we're escorted around the other customers and shown to a table with a superb view of the river and the cliffs above it. Then it dawns on me that Nick's family must own this restaurant. Didn't someone tell me that they own most of Cascade Locks?

"This is nice," I say as I take a menu from the waitress. "Are you going to tell me why you have such a pull with the hostess?"

Nick laughs. "She has worked here for over twenty years. She's now the manager."

"And you own this restaurant."

Nick takes his napkin off the table and nods. "My family does."

He turns to Danny and asks him what he wants to eat, and I watch their exchange, thinking how lucky Danny is to have him. A tiny stab of pain hits my chest and I wonder how Danny would feel if he got to my age and found out that Nick had lied to him. I pray that won't happen because I used to look at my grandmother with the same feeling of adoration that's on Danny's face right now.

We all order hamburgers and get to know each other while we eat. I find out that Nick's had Danny since he was two and his mom died from cancer. His biological father was never part of his life.

After lunch, Danny finds friends to play with and Nick and I sit with our drinks and enjoy the beautiful day. He has been friendly, but distant, and I hope I haven't given him the idea that I'm attracted to him. If I have, I need to back off. I don't want the drama of a romance right now. Finally, I get up the nerve to ask him about Helen.

"Nick, what can you tell me about Helen?"

He takes a swig of beer, looking at me over the bottle. "What would you like to know?"

"Do you have any idea why she won't talk to me?" I play with my napkin folding it into a triangle and smoothing it back out.

"No, it's not like her. She's usually friendly, especially to tourists because they're what keep her in business."

"I have the feeling she really doesn't want to talk about Colleen. She must not have liked her very much. According to Alice, no one in this town did." My heart hurts for Colleen. What would it be like to have everyone in town hate you? What did she do when she realized that they did? Did it make her even more angry?

"Surely not everyone. Alice must be exaggerating."

"I hope so." I take a drink of my iced tea and look out over the water. "Do you think Helen would've been different if I'd gotten to know her before I started asking about Colleen?"

Nick shrugs. "She may have been friendlier. I wish I knew what happened back then. It's kind of like the elephant in the living room. Only it's the monster in the past. No one wants to talk about what happened the night your birth mother left town. I asked my dad about it and he said it's best to leave it alone."

I nod. "That's the impression I'm getting from everyone I talk to, but it makes me more curious. What did she do? Was she that horrible of a person?"

Nick crumples his napkin and puts it on top of his empty burger basket. "No one is all bad. Be careful when you ask around about her. There seem to be some deep-seated dislike of her."

I decide to tell him about the warning left in my room. I know I'm taking a big chance. I don't know this man. He could've left it there to scare me out of town. When I look at his gorgeous brown eyes, I can't quite picture that. Why would he?

"I got a warning to leave town today."

"What? What kind of warning?" He had been leaning back in his chair, enjoying his beer, but now he sits up, his eyes on my face.

"Someone stuck it under the door to my hotel room. It said I need to stop asking questions and leave."

"Did you get hold of the police?"

"No, I'm pretty sure I know who left it."

Nick drains his glass and sets in on the table. "You need to call the police, Natalie. This is serious."

"I think it was Helen, Nick. I can't imagine her actually hurting me." Of course, what do I know? Maybe she's fully capable of hurting me. If she hurt my mother like Gayle thinks, she probably won't hesitate to hurt me, too. I don't mention that thought to Nick, but I'm determined to keep my eye on Helen.

He's shaking his head as he scoots his chair back and stands up. He reaches for my hand. "We've got to call the police. It wasn't Helen, Natalie. I talked to her. She's been in bed all day with a migraine."

Present Day

I get up from my bed, my legs trembling, not wanting to hold my weight. I grab for the end table and almost fall. Damn these legs. They've held me up all my life. Why now, when I still need them, are they giving out on me? I hate getting old alone. Steve's dad has been gone for more than twenty years and now Steve is gone, too. A crushing pain fills my chest at the thought of never seeing my boy again.

I make my way into the living room, holding onto chairs and tables to keep from falling. Magazine's tumble to the floor and I push them under the table with my foot. It feels good to kick them away from me. I'd like to kick the table or sofa, but I know it would only send pain up and down my leg and resemble a kitten kicking at a warehouse.

I've been asleep all morning, but now I have things to do. I look around. What was I going to do? There was something important, but I can't remember what.

Panic seizes me, and I want to crawl back into bed and sleep the rest of the day, but I know I need to keep going.

I fumble through a stack of books on my end table and pick up a photo album that has been there for years. I sit hard on my chair and feel the jarring pain down to my knees. I open the book on my lap. The pictures are old and curling at the corners. My fingers tremble as I run them over the fading colors. I turn the pages, continuing to caress the pictures as I watch the progression of time in them.

My son Steve, and Colleen Winters smile at me from beside the Sweet Onion Café in 1990. "She was such a pretty girl. Such a beauty. It's too bad she wasn't pretty on the inside." I rock back and forth on my chair. "No, she was a bad girl. It's her fault Steve went to jail. If only Colleen hadn't come back to town. If only she hadn't done the things she did.

I think back to the night she died. I never told anyone, kept my secret all these years. I shake my head, trying to clear the cobwebs. "That needs to stay in the past. I'll never tell anyone what happened that night. I could lose so much if anyone ever found out."

The phone rings and I think about ignoring it, but I know it won't do any good. I reach over and pick it up.

There is silence on the other end of the phone, and then a voice I recognize very well says, "You know what you have to do, Alice. She's asking too many questions. Get rid of her."

Without answering, I put the phone down and tears pool in my eyes and run down my cheeks. I hold the photo album close to my heart, letting the tears fall. "Why have I let things go so long? I need to clean up this mess before things get into the wrong hands."

I swipe at my eyes with the sleeve of my faded pink sweatshirt and lay the photo album down next to me. With new resolve, I get up and make my way slowly to the back room, to the box that I left there many years ago and the secrets it holds.

CHAPTER 11: NATALIE

Present Day

Nick and I argue quietly as we leave the restaurant. I don't want to involve the police. "It's not like it was a threat to do violence, Nick. What are the police going to do?"

Nick has his phone out ready to dial 911. He puts it back in his pocket. "You're right, but I don't like this. Why would someone threaten you? You haven't been here long enough to make enemies."

Danny climbs up on a stone wall and jumps off. I watch him for a minute, wishing I could feel that carefree. "Something happened back before Colleen went missing, something that people in this town don't want to remember. My coming here is stirring them up, making them remember."

"Threats are a drastic way of showing their fear."

I nod, agreeing with him. "If something else happens, I'll call the police, I promise."

Nick doesn't look happy, but he nods and turns to Danny. "We'd better get home."

Danny jumps down from the ledge one more time. "Will we see you tomorrow?" he asks me.

I smile and ruffle his hair. "I'm not sure what I'm doing tomorrow."

"I know what I'm doing. I'm going to work with Dad."

Nick frowns at him. "You are? Since when?"

"Since you fired my babysitter."

I laugh and tell them goodbye and head to my room. As I insert my keycard, I wonder what I'll find behind the door. Will there be another threat? I know I'm psyching myself out, but I can't seem to stop.

The door opens, and I flip on the light, looking around. Nothing. No paper on the floor with threats on it. No scary person waiting in the bathroom to jump out and grab me. I open the closet to make sure I'm alone and it's empty except for my suitcase. I breathe a sigh of relief and put my bag down on the bed.

I spend what's left of the afternoon searching on my computer for Colleen, hoping I missed something and she's alive and well somewhere, but nothing comes up. Feeling depressed, I give in to the sleep that's tugging at me and take a nap.

Later I wake up and feel much better. I head to the pizza restaurant for dinner, wishing I didn't have to eat alone. When I finish, after drinking wine and talking to the owner for a couple hours, I head back to the hotel.

It's still light outside. I could go for a walk, but I've had a long day and decide to go to bed and read. The words blur and I'm almost asleep when the phone next to the bed rings. My heart pounds. I haven't given out this number. I don't even know this number. I sit up and scramble for the light, then pick up the phone and say hello. Nothing. No answering hello, no sorry, wrong number, no nothing but heavy breathing.

"Who is this?"

Click.

I slam the phone down on the receiver, then sit for a long time staring at it. What have I done? My heart is pounding. I grab a pillow and hold it against me. Then I sit against the headboard for the rest of the night, afraid to go to sleep.

The next morning I'm up early glad for daylight when the threats of the night before don't seem quite as scary.

I decide to go for a walk and clear my brain. There are boats out on the river and I hear an airplane overhead. I look up and let the sun warm my face. The day is glorious just like the one before. I wonder how long the warm weather will hold. Is Cascade Locks allotted a certain amount of sun before it rains again? I laugh at myself. I've come here thinking it will rain all the time, but I'm starting to realize I've heard too many stories of a rainy northwest.

Two people jog towards me on the path. I move over to let them pass and recognize Gayle Woods. Without thinking, I put out my hand to stop her, something I would never do in Florida. "Gayle."

She stops short and the man with her keeps going, realizes she's not with him, and doubles back. "Oh hello," Gayle says. She doesn't smile, she looks at me with her large white sunglasses hiding her eyes.

"It's a beautiful morning for a jog."

"Yes, it is. Ben and I jog every morning." She motions to the man who has stopped beside her. "This is my husband, Ben." Then she gestures to me. "This is Natalie. We met yesterday in the Sweet Onion."

Ben reaches out and shakes my hand. He's a good-looking older man with light brown hair and a pleasant face. His eyes are covered with sunglasses and I wish he would take them off, so I could see them. My heart thumps. Could he be my father?

"It's nice to meet you." He releases my hand and gives me one of those 'what can you do?' smiles. "Gayle never sees a stranger."

Gayle looks at him. I get the feeling that she's not happy to see me. What happened to the friendly woman who just yesterday wanted to help me find my birth mother?

I'm starting to feel uncomfortable with her silence and decide to move on, but Ben doesn't seem to feel the tension. He asks, "Are you going to be here this weekend? It's our big Sternwheeler Days celebration." Ben puts his arm around Gayle and gives her shoulder a squeeze.

"What is that?" I ask him.

"It's the town's celebration of the return of the Sternwheeler after winter. We have live music, dancing, games, craft vendors and food. There's even a beer garden."

I can tell that Ben is all for the beer garden.

"Yes, you need to stay and enjoy the weekend with us. How long are you planning to be here?" Gayle's words are friendly enough, but the tone of her voice reminds me of the movie, Frozen. I expect to look at the ground and find ice forming everywhere. What's with her? She was so friendly yesterday. I give a mental head shake.

Gayle knows that I'm here looking for Colleen, but I get the idea that she doesn't want Ben to know that she knows. "I'll be here for a while. It sounds like a fun weekend."

They say goodbye and continue their jog and I'm left wondering why Gayle doesn't want her husband to know that she and I talked about Colleen yesterday. I'm beginning to think that this town has more than its share of secrets. At first, it seems like the movie, The Stepford Wives, where everything is wonderful and perfect on the outside, but you scratch the surface at all and the ugly shows through.

Back at the hotel, the receptionist, the girl with the tattoo who checked me in, stops me as I head for my room. "Oh, hey, someone left this here for you." She hands me an envelope.

"Who left it?"

"I'm not sure. It was lying on the desk when I came in this morning."

She holds it out to me, and I take it. My hands are shaking. Who would have left me a letter? Is it another threat? Do I even want to open it? "So, you don't have any idea of who left it?"

The receptionist, whose name tag reads, Jill Weatherspoon, gives me a 'no such luck' smile and walks back to her computer. "No, sorry."

I don't want to open it in the lobby where whoever left it could walk by and see my reaction. I step outside into the sunshine, which feels like my safe place right now. Outside there are people strolling around, heading for the Bridgeside Restaurant for breakfast. The cleaning crew is milling around, pushing their carts and I can hear the small wheels clatter on the pavement as they move from one room to another.

My hands are trembling as I open the envelope. Inside is a piece of lined notebook paper. The words are written in a shaky hand and say, *we need to talk. Come to my house at 11am. Don't tell anyone. Alice*

I suck in my breath. What changed between yesterday and today? Why does she want to talk to me now? I don't know, but I'll be there. Maybe now she'll be willing to give me the answers I need.

Present Day

The next morning as I get ready for work, I wonder what I'm going to do with Danny since I fired his babysitter. It's not conceivable to take him to work with me every day for the rest of the summer. "Thanks a lot, Chloe." Not that I'd want to have Chloe babysit again. I shudder at the thought of what could have happened the day before on her watch. I need a sitter, or I'll have to take Danny to work with me.

I think about my growing attraction to Natalie. What should I do? Take the coward's way out and do nothing? I grimace at my reflection in the mirror as I run the razor over my face. "Stay away from her. That's the best thing to do."

Danny walks into the bathroom in his Pokémon jammies and leans against my leg. "'Morning, Dad."

I lean down and rub his back. "Good morning, son."

"Can I spend the day with Natalie?" Danny looks up with a hopeful look on his face.

"What? No. Natalie isn't here to babysit you."

"But I like her."

Like father, like son, I think, but we don't need more complications in our life. And how do you explain that to a six-year-old?

"Natalie has plans today, I'm sure." I glance at the frown on my son's face and sigh. "Why don't you come to work with me? Maybe Granddad will be at the office and he can take you out on the job site for a while."

"Really?" Danny jumps off the toilet. "That's way cool. Will you call and ask him?"

"Sure. Go get dressed and I'll give him a call. Then we can get breakfast."

I smile as Danny runs from the room, shouting orders as he goes. "Tell Granddad I'll work too. I can use a hammer. He showed me how to do it without hitting my thumb. Grandad says that's important."

"Yeah, that's pretty important." I shake my head, amused at his quick change of attitude and run a comb through my hair and straighten up the bathroom.

I call my dad's cell phone, but he doesn't answer, so I leave a message. Then Danny and I head to the office. Dad's not there, so I call him again. This time he picks up, and he agrees to take Danny for the afternoon. "Why don't the three of us have lunch together? We haven't done that in a long time."

I agree, thinking we can catch up on business and Danny will love spending more time with his granddad.

Danny and I stay at the office and work until lunch, then we get in the pickup and head across the bridge to Stevenson, Washington. We're meeting Jonas at a small Mexican restaurant there.

It's a ten-minute drive across the Bridge of the Gods from Cascade Locks to Stevenson, and Jonas's pickup is parked outside when we arrive.

"Can I have a pork burrito, Dad?" Danny's newest favorite food is pork.

"Sure."

"And a Coke?"

I open the door of the restaurant and let Danny walk in ahead of me. "Sure. Anything else?"

Danny grins. "Maybe dessert?"

Jonas is at a table near the front window and we wave and join him. "Hey, Danny."

"Granddad." Danny runs to him and gives him a big hug. "Dad says I can have a pork burrito and use the hammer this afternoon on the job site."

"Whoa, little man. I didn't say you could use the hammer. You said you could."

"Oh."

Jonas laughs and pulls Danny in for a hug. "We'll talk about the hammer, okay?"

Over lunch, Dad and I discuss business while Danny plays a game on his Nintendo Switch. We're almost finished when Jonas says, "So what's up with you having lunch yesterday with that girl?"

I toss my napkin on the table. So that's what this lunch is all about. "How did you know that?"

Jonas shrugs. "I know everything."

"She saved Danny from a bad fall. He wanted to take her to lunch as a sort of thank-you."

Danny looks up from his game. "I was going over the edge of the cliff and she grabbed me." He's so matter of fact about it that it makes us both chuckle. "I gotta use the bathroom, Dad." He jumps up and heads to the toilet.

Jonas leans across the table and speaks in a low voice. "You need to listen to my advice, Nick. Stay away from her."

"What's going on, Dad? You keep saying Colleen wasn't a good person, but you can't know what kind of a person Natalie is. Colleen didn't raise her."

Jonas finishes his lunch and stands up, throwing his napkin on the table. He reaches for his wallet and pulls out a few bills. "Let's just say there are things that happened in Cascade Locks a long time ago that don't need to be remembered. If Natalie keeps digging, she's going to dig up dirt on some prominent families and it won't be good for anybody."

"Like our family?" I add my money to the check for our food. I'm beginning to realize that my father has some buried secrets he doesn't want to let out. That thought makes me feel nauseous. What happened to make him so worried?

"Like a lot of families, Nick."

The door behind us opens and a teenage boy rushes in. The restaurant owner looks up when the kid calls his name. "Hey Carl, did you hear there's something bad going on in Cascade Locks?"

"What?" The man named Carl looks up from the receipts in his hand.

"Dunno, but there are sirens going off and I can see fire trucks and police cars everywhere across the river. Something big, I'd guess."

CHAPTER 13: COLLEEN

Thirty years ago

When I came to, the Sheriff demanded my parent's names and phone number. I didn't want to give it to him, but I was afraid to tell him no, so I gave in.

Jose's dad sat on the front step, his head in his hands. His wife peeked out of the trailer. He said something to her in Spanish that I didn't understand, his words soft and careful, and she went back inside.

Everardo sat next to his dad, his arm around him. Tears ran down their faces. Everardo's fists were doubled up, ready to do battle. The veins in his arms stood out, red and angry, and I hoped he'd go looking for Larry White and Steve Perkins.

Since my house wasn't far away, my mother came on foot, her nightgown peeking out from under her old black raincoat. She said my name and I ran to her and slipped into her arms. She rocked me back and forth, murmuring words of comfort.

"What happened, baby?" she asked, as she pulled away and brushed my hair back from my face.

"Oh, Mama." I burst into tears again and she held me, her arms wrapped tight around me. She hugged me close, and then the Sheriff took her aside to talk to her. I heard him say 'you need to take her to the hospital', and I shook my head. "No."

"You find those two, Sheriff, and you put them in jail for what they did to my Colleen and that nice Mexican boy." Mama's voice was husky with tears. "You hear me, Sheriff?"

The Sheriff told us he'd be by in the morning to talk to me. My mother nodded and put her arm around me, and we headed home.

"Those rotten bastards. We need to get you to the hospital. Make sure you're all right."

"No, Mama, I don't want to go. I just want to go home." I was so exhausted I felt like I might fall. I wanted to lie down in the street and go to sleep and never wake up again. I didn't want to live in a world without Jose.

"You need to see a doctor, Colleen. Who knows what kind of diseases those SOB's may carry?"

"Tomorrow, Mama, I'll go tomorrow. I can't tonight." Tears ran down my cheeks and she gave in. Mama had never been able to withstand my tears.

We walked the rest of the way home in silence. Mama took her arm off my shoulder and pushed her hand into my back, urging me to walk faster. I stumbled and she slowed down, matching her stride to mine. If I wasn't so upset about Jose, I would worry about her. But right then, all I could think about was Jose. I put a hand up to my chest and felt the fast beating of my heart. I knew it was my fault they killed him. It was all my fault.

Our house was dark and for the first time, I was relieved that my father was off somewhere in a drunken stupor every night. I didn't know what he'd do when he heard what happened, but I knew if he was drunk, it would be ten times worse.

Mama opened the kitchen door and we walked in. She went to the sink and ran hot water. "Sit down, Colleen. I want to clean the scrapes on your arms and legs."

I looked down at my legs and saw blood trickling down my left one from the deep scratches Steve Perkins made on my skin. There were scrapes on my arms and I gingerly touched my face and my fingers came away with blood on them. I sat at the table and she knelt next to me, placing the soft, cool cloth on my scrapes.

Suddenly, the overhead light came on and my father barged into the room, swearing like a sailor. "What the hell happened to her? Run off again, girl? Your poor mother works all the time and she don't need to be up all-night taking care of the likes of you."

He swung his fist, missing me by a mile, but I ducked and squealed. Mama jumped up and steered him into a chair. "Sit down, Leroy. It's not what you think."

"Then what the hell is it? You find her out doing the nasty with that Mexican kid?" He started to rise like he was coming after me, but Mama grabbed his hand.

"No! Sit down, Leroy. We need to talk."

My father sat and put his head in his hand. "Get me some aspirin, Nita. My head's killing me."

I hated my father. I hated him because he drank all the time. I hated him because Mama worked her butt off for our family, and he sat in a bar all day telling his drunken friends what a good woman he had.

"Why don't you get up and get it yourself?"

My father came up from the table with a roar. Mama got between us, but he swiped her away like a fly that was buzzing around his head. "You little..."

Before he could say more, Mama screamed, "don't Leroy. She's been raped."

If Mama thought that would calm him down, she failed. But it did shut him up. He stood there for five seconds, his mouth gapping open like some sort of blowfish, and his bloodshot eyes bulging out. Then he sank onto the kitchen chair and burst into tears. Deep sobs shook his large body.

I looked at Mama, who didn't take her eyes off him. When he lifted his head, all he said was, "who did it?" And I trembled at the deadly sober tone of his voice.

"That Larry White and his friend, Steve Perkins, that's who." Mama leaned against the sink and rubbed her hands over her face. She had tears in her eyes and for the first time since I let the sheriff think that I'd been raped, I felt bad about it. I hadn't thought about how much pain it would cause my mama. "They can't get away with this, Leroy."

"You're damn right about that." My father stood and left the room.

"Mama?" I started to tell her that I really wasn't raped, that they just tried to rape me. But the words wouldn't come out.

"It's okay, darlin'. Let's get you into the tub. A nice warm soak will do you good. And then I'll give you something to help you sleep."

She helped me into the bathroom and ran the tub full of hot water. She put in her favorite rose bubble bath and the fragrance filled the small room. She reached into the medicine cabinet and took out a prescription bottle and shook out two pills and handed them to me with a glass of water. Then she touched my arm and left the bathroom. I took off my clothes and threw them in the trash, including Helen's sweater.

Shivers ran up and down my body. The hot water hurt as I slid into the tub. I needed it to be hot, as hot as possible. I wanted every centimeter of my skin cleansed from Steve's touch. I picked up a washcloth and scrubbed at my skin until it was red and raw. Then I leaned back and closed my eyes, wishing I'd never left the house. I wished that Jose was alive. Why had this happened? How could they do this to Jose?

I couldn't think about what might've happened to me. I didn't want to remember the feel of Steve's hands all over me, squeezing and pinching places he shouldn't be touching, so I concentrated on Jose.

The tears, which hadn't been far away since I found out about my boyfriend, began again, and I leaned over and sobbed into my washcloth. I cried until the water turned cold and I had to add more hot water.

After a while, I heard a commotion outside the bathroom; my parents raised voices and a door slammed. I got out of the tub and grabbed a towel, drying my body. Then I pulled my robe off the hook on the door and put it around me.

When I got into the living room, Mama sat on the sofa looking out the window at the black night. The night light outside had been burnt out for months. "Mama?"

She turned to me her eyes red from crying. "Go get into bed, baby girl."

"Where's dad?"

"He's gone to help find those boys. We talked to the sheriff and he said they haven't found them yet."

"Dad wouldn't do anything stupid, would he?"

"Like shoot the SOB's?"

I couldn't believe my mother would think it's okay for Dad to take the law into his own hands. Even though Larry and Steve deserved what they got, Dad would go to jail forever if he shot them.

I ran to the closet where he kept his rifle. When I opened it, the rifle was gone. "Mama, Dad's taken his rifle."

"I know," she whispered. "God help him."

Present Day

At exactly eleven o'clock the next morning I'm at Alice's door. I knock on the door frame. "Alice?"

I can't hear anything from inside, so I knock again. A few minutes later, when I still haven't raised her, I reach for the knob. It turns easily in my hand, and I lift on the door to open it.

The living room looks the same as it did last time I was there. The only thing missing is Alice. I call her name and hear a sound from the back of the house. "Coming," she says as she shuffles down the small hallway pushing a walker. "Sorry, I didn't hear you come in." She pushes a strand of white hair behind her ear.

"I knocked."

She nods and makes her way slowly to the sofa where she plops down, breathing hard from the exertion. "I was in the bathroom." She pats the sofa. "Sit down. We need to talk."

I sit beside her, wishing I could open a window and air

the place out. I'm hoping that she's going to tell me something about my mother. "Why did you want to see me?"

Alice sits back and closes her eyes. "I've been thinking a lot about what you asked me." She opens her eyes and gives me a direct look. "And I think it's time to tell Colleen's story."

My heart thuds inside me. I've never had a heart attack, but I wonder if this is what it feels like. For a second or two I can't breathe. Is this real? Is she finally going to tell me about my birth mother?

Alice leans back and rests her hands on her stomach. She closes her eyes again and begins talking in a soft voice.

"Colleen was a troubled girl. She didn't follow the rules her folks had at home. Nor did she do well in school. Most of the people who knew her thought her problems were because her father molested her. He wasn't a good man.

"She played hard and drank too much, did drugs and ended up leaving town when she was in high school. Many of us thought she was pregnant, but we never heard of a baby until she had you and that was a few years later."

It's so hot in her house. I can smell the garbage can next to her chair. I think I'm going to faint. Alice quits talking and takes a swig of water that has been sitting there for who knows how long. She makes a face and asks me to get her a fresh glass with ice.

I get up and go into the kitchen and it's even worse than the living room. There are dishes piled in the sink, on the counters and on the table, which also has papers and food along with old coffee pots, pots and pans and dishes. There are flies buzzing the dried-out food, and I cover my mouth and nose as I try to find a glass clean enough to put water in.

"There's cold water in the fridge," she yells from the living room.

With a feeling of trepidation, I open the refrigerator door. It's not as bad as I assumed it would be, but it smells awful, like broccoli that has been left too long. I take the pitcher out and pour water into a glass I find in the cupboard. Then I look in the freezer for ice. There's an old-fashioned ice tray with a couple cubes in it which I add to the glass before making my way back into the living room.

When I hand it to Alice she says, "Don't you want a drink?"

"No thanks. I'm fine." My throat is so dry it feels like I've been inhaling sand, but I'm afraid to drink out of anything in this house. I sit back down on the sofa and wait for her to finish her story.

She takes a long drink and puts the glass on the end table next to three others. She clears her throat. "So, where was I? Oh, I know, Colleen left here and was gone for a couple years. Then she came back. She went to work for her sister at the café. By that time both of her parents had died.

"Colleen was angry at everyone, especially Helen. She set out to break Helen and Jonas up. After she did that, she broke up every marriage she could. Finally, she and Helen had a huge fight that ended with Helen being hurt badly. Colleen ran off again and no one has seen her since." She took another drink of water.

"Why was she mad at everyone?"

Alice squirms. "She blamed her sister and father for her mother's death. Then she blamed the folks in town because her mom worked so hard at that café and they quit going. She had to close it for a while, and it did her in."

We sit in silence for a couple minutes. "That's it? No one looked for Colleen? Did anyone call the police?"

Alice shrugs. "What could they do? She took her clothes and personal items and left. She didn't pay her last month's rent. We figured she was embarrassed because of her fight with Helen and took off again." She's quiet for a few minutes, and then she says, "I've heard rumors that she went to California with some guy. What happened after that is anybody's guess."

I look at her. Something about her story doesn't ring true, but I don't know what it is. Then it hits me. "Alice, if that's true, why were you so scared the first time I came here to talk to you? Why didn't you want to tell me about Colleen?"

She shrugs. "I hated to disappoint you."

"I don't believe you. That's a good story, but there's more to it, isn't there? If Colleen had a fight with Helen and ran off why does her sister hate her? Why won't Helen talk to me? Why did some woman I don't know stop me and tell me that Helen killed my mother?"

Alice's eyes almost pop out of her sockets. "Who told you that?"

I ignore her question. "Something happened to Colleen Winters. Something that neither you or Helen want to talk about. What is it? Why are you keeping the truth from me?" My hands are shaking, and I try to control my anger, but I know she's keeping something from me. "Will you at least tell me why Leona took me from her in the first place?"

Alice takes her glasses off and wipes her eyes with her hand. Then she puts them back on and sighs. "Leona should have told you the truth. I told her she should, but she thought it better to make up those lies." She stops talking and looks down at her hands. "I asked Leona to take you away. You needed a better life than what Colleen could give you."

I'm amazed by her confession. "Why did Colleen let me go? Don't most mothers fight to keep their children? Even bad mothers I've known want to keep their children with them. Why did she give me to Leona?"

Alice reaches out and touches my hand. It's a soft, hesitant touch and she removes her hand from mine so fast I wonder if I imagined it. "Some women shouldn't have children, Natalie. Colleen was one of them. All she could think about was having you and getting her figure back, so she could go out and party again."

I feel my heart breaking for that little baby girl who wasn't wanted. Tears form in my eyes and slip down my face. I flick them away. Do you ever get over feeling like you were an imposition to your own mother? Not wanted, not loved, something to be rid of like yesterday's trash. I close my eyes and try to get a grip on my emotions. I don't want to cry in front of Alice. I will hold the tears until I'm alone again.

"So, she just handed me over to Leona? How did she even know her?"

Alice sighs and I can tell she's getting tired. "Leona was my friend. I knew she'd wanted a child for a long time, so I arranged the adoption for Colleen."

I remember the contract Leona signed and the money that exchanged hands. "What did Colleen do with the ten thousand dollars Leona paid her for me?"

Alice looks surprised and says quickly, too quickly. "I don't know." She stands up on shaky legs and for a second, I think she's going to fall back onto the sofa, but she gets her bearings. "I think it's time for you to go." She walks to the door and pulls it open without a struggle.

I stand up too, knowing I have a lot to think about. "Why did she try so hard to ruin the reputations of the men in this town?"

"I don't have the answers to that. I've told you everything I know; now you need to leave. Leave my house, leave town, and go back to Florida. There's nothing for you here."

"Why don't you want me to find Colleen?"

"I don't know where she is. She could be in another country by now. All I know is, she's not here." Alice opens the door wider. "Now, please go. I'm tired."

I walk past her and out the door. I can see how tired she is from our talk. Sweat trickles down my back and the cooler air outside sends a chill over my skin. Her house felt like a greenhouse---a smelly greenhouse. I dig an elastic band out of my bag and pull my long hair back into a ponytail, then swirl it into a knot, loving the feel of the cooler air on my neck.

I walk back towards WaNaPa Street, thinking about Alice and Colleen. The hurt is still there, like a vacuum inside of me. I feel abandoned again, like I did when I found out Leona lied to me. Now I find out that Colleen gave me away, so she could continue with her life as a party girl. That ten thousand dollars gave her a lot of money to party with. It's nice that I could be born so she could sell me for drugs and alcohol.

There's a coffee place on the next block, and I go over and buy an iced latte. I feel shaky after my talk with Alice, so I find a chair outside on the patio and decide to sit next to a table. I have so much to think about.

The town is unusually quiet, and I wonder where everyone is, thankful that I can sit where it's quiet and think. As far as I know, all the hotels and campgrounds are full. I look up at the teenage boy who is sweeping off the patio and straightening chairs. "Where is everyone?"

He shrugs. "Most of the tourists are heading to the river. The wind is supposed to pick up this afternoon. The locals are probably getting ready for the Sternwheeler Days, and there was a big party last night at the campground. They may be still sleeping it off. Either that or they're out hiking."

"It's so quiet. Is this what it's like in the winter?"

He stops sweeping and leans on the broom. "Nah, it's rea---lly quiet in the winter." He draws out the really.

"What do you do for fun in the winter?"

"Not much. Go to Hood River or Portland to the movies, play video games." He finishes sweeping and says, "Can I get you anything else?"

"No, thanks, I'm good." I finish my latte and give him the glass.

I decide to go for a hike. I didn't bring hiking boots, but I do have tennis shoes, so I can wear them. I start walking towards the hotel, lost in thought about Alice and Colleen. I see a white blur ahead of me and realize it's a woman on a bike. She has long white hair tied back in a ponytail and I'm pretty sure it's Helen. I wonder where she's going at such a fast clip, when I see her turn onto Venture St.

Since that's where Alice lives, I decide to follow. As far as I know, Helen could live on the same street. But I have nothing better to do, except spend time thinking about Colleen---which is something I want to put off because my mind keeps going around in circles--- so I walk back up the street where Alice lives. When I get to her house, sure enough the bike is leaning up against the sagging porch.

I want to eavesdrop to see what Helen was in such a hurry to tell Alice. I try not to make a sound as I creep up on the porch and approach the door. Luckily for me, Helen has left it partially open and I can hear her talking to Alice inside. I glance around to make sure none of Alice's neighbors are around, and then I lean my head close to the door.

Alice is talking, her creaky old voice filled with tension.

"I don't have a choice, Helen. You get her to stop asking questions and I won't tell what I know."

"I don't care who you tell." Helen is yelling at Alice, and I peek inside and see her standing over the old lady with her fist knotted and a look of loathing on her face.

"Of course, you do. Now get out of here before I call the police myself."

I step back, and the door of Alice's house opens and Helen storms out. "You can't do this, Alice Perkins. I will see you in hell first," she screams as she grabs her bike and flies down the road.

"Helen, stop!" I run after her, but she's too fast and I can't keep up.

Present Day

Heat rises from the cement sidewalk as I walk towards my hotel. I'm sweating and think longingly of the swimming pool. Maybe I should go for a swim and decide what to do next.

A thought nags at me. Alice said my mother cleaned out her rental when she left. I didn't think to ask her who Colleen was renting from, but I'm guessing it was Jonas since his family seems to own everything in Cascade Locks. I decide to go ask him if he rented to Colleen, hoping he'll talk to me today.

I haven't heard from Nick since I left his office yesterday, so I assume he couldn't talk his dad into telling me what he knows about Colleen.

I think about walking back to get my car because then I can ride in air conditioning, letting the cool air blow over my face and cool my body. I decide to walk instead, hoping the wind will pick up like the boy at the coffee place said it would. Down by the water the windsurfers and kite boarders are getting their boards ready to get out on the water. The bright colored sails add a pop of color to the deep blue of the river.

A tugboat, pushing a load of gravel down the river catches my attention. I wonder what else they transport this way.

Traffic on WaNaPa Street has picked up, and the ice cream spot, the East Wind Drive In, has several people waiting in line for something to eat. I promise myself an ice cream cone on the way back.

It takes longer than I thought to walk the length of the town to Forest Lane. I'm regretting not bringing my car when I see Jonas's office building ahead of me. There aren't any pickups outside, and I feel a little disappointed. I didn't come to see Nick, but deep down I must've hoped I would.

The door to the office is closed, and I walk up the steps planning to open it and enter. Before I can, the door flies open and Helen storms out. She runs around the building with me on her heels.

"Helen, wait a minute. What's going on?"

She doesn't answer. Instead she grabs her bike, which she'd left leaning against the side of the building and climbs on. I run around in front of her. "What's wrong? I saw you at Alice's. Why did you leave angry?"

Her eyes narrow and shoot daggers at me. "Stay.Out-.Of.My.Business. You've already stirred up enough trouble."

"What did I do? What trouble? Please, you have to talk to me some time. Alice told me you fought with Colleen the night she left town. What did you fight about?"

"I don't have to tell you anything. Get out of my way." She jerks the handlebars and rides off, her white ponytail flipping around her shoulders.

"She's in a good mood," a voice behind me says and I

turn around to see Jenna, the receptionist I talked to the day before standing on the front porch watching Helen cycle away.

"Do you know what's up with her?"

"Not a clue. She came storming in here saying she had to talk to Jonas. I told her he's out on a job and she blew up, said she's tired of everyone protecting him and took off."

She turns toward the office door. "Come on in, I'll get us a cold drink. It's hotter than Hades out here. I hear the wind is supposed to kick up soon."

I follow her into the office and look around. I didn't pay attention to the outer office when I was here before. I was too intent on my visit---wanting to talk to Jonas---and Nick.

Their office is beautiful with natural wood walls and soft leather furniture. Jenna's desk is a walnut L-shape with built in shelves. What a great place to work.

Jenna goes into a room next to Nick's office and asks what I'd like. I ask for bottled water and she grabs two and brings them back to the front office. She hands me the water and sits down on the sofa. "Come sit down."

I sit on the other end of the sofa and uncap my water, taking a long drink. "Mmm, thanks, I needed that."

"So, what's going on with Helen? She's usually so calm and easy going."

"Helen is?"

Jenna chuckles. "Yeah, when I see her, she is. But I've only worked here a few months, and she doesn't come in that often." She crosses her legs and tugs at her jeans skirt.

"I don't know what's going on. She hasn't been friendly to me since I arrived in town." In fact, she's been hostile, but I don't tell Jenna that.

"Nick said you're here looking for your birth mother.

Must be hard to not have known the woman who gave you birth." She tips her water up and takes a swallow.

Some mother, I think. She sold me, her own baby, for ten thousand dollars and then went out to play. A part of me wonders why I even care what happened to her. She sure didn't care what happened to me. "Are you from here?"

Jenna is attractive, and I find myself wondering if Nick thinks so, which is crazy since Nick and I are from the opposite sides of the country, and it really shouldn't matter what he thinks. Besides, I'm sure he has lots of women who are interested in him.

"No, my husband and I came out west on vacation about three years ago. We liked it so much we moved here. Jason teaches windsurfing and kite boarding lessons in the summer and skiing in the winter. And I was lucky enough to get a job here. I really like Nick; he's a great guy to work for."

A tiny part of me is happy to hear she's married. I tell myself I'm pathetic. "And Jonas?"

"He's okay. Wound a little tight, if you know what I mean. I'm a little surprised that he's Nick's dad."

"Have you met Nick's mom?"

Jenna shakes her head. Today her black hair is pulled back into a braid. "No, as far as I know she lives in Portland and does her best to stay away from Jonas. That's what Nick told me. Hey, I'm sure you didn't stop in to visit with me. Were you looking for Nick?"

"No, I wanted to talk to Jonas."

"Hmm, he's popular today. I wonder if that's why he offered to go to the job site. They're working on a house in Lyle. It's about forty miles away across the river in Washington and they don't get great cell service up there."

"Who else is looking for him?"

"An old lady named Alice Perkins keeps calling here demanding to talk to him."

"Really?"

"Yeah, you know her?"

"We've met."

"And Nick has Danny today. I hear he had to fire Danny's babysitter. Poor guy. He has quite a time finding someone to stay with the little guy."

I drain my bottle of water. "How come? He seems like a good kid."

"Oh, he is. But Nick's picky about who he hires. He was kicking himself this morning about trusting the last one. Apparently, she almost let Danny fall in the river."

I nod, thinking about how he'd slipped and if I hadn't been standing right there, what might have happened.

The phone rings and Jenna gets up to answer it. "Hey Jonas. Things are quiet here. You've had some visitors and phone calls. Alice Perkins called seven times. Helen came by wanting to talk to you. She seemed pretty upset about something. And Natalie is here." She smiles at me, and then Jonas must've said something because she turns away. "No, of course I haven't let anyone in your office. You know I wouldn't do that."

They talk for a couple minutes and she finally puts the phone down. "Well, he's not in the best of moods today. Hope Nick comes back before he gets here."

"What did he say when you told him I was here?" I stand up to leave, knowing she probably has work to do.

"You don't want to know. The man can swear. But I'm not sure it was because you were here, or because Helen was. He didn't seem happy about either. Sorry."

I tell her goodbye and head back to town. The wind has come up a bit and I think I hear a siren as I walk. I wonder what the siren's for. It gets louder as I near town. I hurry my steps and soon I'm back on WaNaPa Street. Looking east I see fire trucks heading toward the west end of town.

"What's burning?" I ask a man standing on the sidewalk looking towards the hotel where I'm staying. The smell of smoke is intense, and I put my hand over my nose.

"I heard it's the Best Western."

"The hotel?" My heart sinks. "I hope my room's okay."

"They said it's on the second floor, near the elevator." He has his hand up shading his eyes. Smoke rises from the hotel in plumes of grey and black.

"No! My room is on the second floor." I start running and hear him yelling behind me. I don't stop. Did I leave my picture of Colleen in my room? Oh, dear God, I hope not.

"They aren't going to let you in."

I know that, but I keep running. There are people standing around watching as the smoke curls and rises into the sky. The fire department truck is sitting in the parking lot. There are firemen everywhere, trying to put out the flames. Police and firemen are trying to keep people away from the hotel. As I approach, a young man holds his hand out in front of me. "Sorry Miss, but you can't come closer. We don't want anyone getting hurt."

I stand to one side to watch with a group of people who are talking about their iPads and laptops still inside the structure. "My boss is going to kill me if I lose another laptop," a woman a little younger than me says. She's biting her lip and watching the firemen trying to put out the flames.

"What's going on?" A voice next to me asks and I realize it's Gayle Woods.

"Looks like the hotel caught on fire. I wonder what

started it." I look at her and realize she's mesmerized by the fire. There's a frown between her eyes.

"Wow. There hasn't been a real fire in Cascade Locks in a few years."

I turn to her. "A real fire?"

She nods. "Yeah, the firemen have burned down old houses as a drill, but I don't think there have been any accidental fires for a while. This isn't good."

"It wasn't accidental." A young man wearing khaki shorts and a white Polo shirt with flip flops on his feet walks up closer to us. "I heard it was set deliberately."

Gayle looks at him. "Really? Who would do that?"

He shrugs. "Don't know, but whoever it was meant business. That whole wing of the hotel is going up in smoke." He raises his hand and I can see that he's right. And my heart sinks when I realize that it's the part of the hotel where I am staying.

Without thinking I take off running towards the hotel. My laptop and Colleen's picture are still in my room. I hear Gayle's voice yelling at me to stop, but I keep running.

At the entrance closest to my room a fireman tries to stop me, but I fly past him. He reaches out but he can't stop me.

"Miss, you can't go in there."

I ignore him and grab hold of the door. The hallway is full of smoke, but my room is close to the door and I make it without any problems except that the air is so thick with smoke, I start coughing and struggling to breathe.

To my surprise, my keycard works, and the door opens easily. I prop open the door with a trash can. The only light is from the window and the sliding glass door. I grab my laptop. The picture is on my dresser and I grab it and put it in my pocket. I only have a few minutes before the smoke will force me out of the building. I grab everything I can and stuff it into my bag.

My eyes are stinging from the smoke and my throat hurts. I pick up a few things from off the vanity and turn to the door. Someone is standing in the hall. I feel relieved that help has come. But instead of helping me, they shove the door closed in my face. I reach out and try to pull it open, but it doesn't budge. I slam my fist against it and scream, "let me out."

My heart pounds. Someone locked me in my room. I'm choking and feeling disoriented. I head back into the bathroom for a wet washcloth to put over my nose, when a blast rocks the building and I'm thrown against the door.

CHAPTER 16: HELEN

Present Day

I smell smoke the minute I hit WaNaPa Street. I look around, hoping it isn't my house or café. Luckily for me, it's the Best Western Hotel. I breathe a sigh of relief, and then wonder what caused the fire. People are slowing down to gawk as they drive by, causing traffic to crawl through town. The street is loaded with pedestrians trying to get a better look. Smoke is rising from the building, curling in the air like feathers.

The town is crazy with tourists and now they will have to find someplace else to stay. I ride to my café and leave my bike behind it in the area near the shed where I store all the paper products for the café, and everything else I don't have room for.

I'm so mad at Jonas I could shoot him. Why is he hiding from me? What did he tell Alice about the night Colleen left? What do they know that I don't?

Alice called me earlier and told me she needed to see me. That it was urgent. I rode over on my bike during my lunch break and she met me at the door, urging me inside.

"We've got to do something about Natalie before she digs up all the old stories about Colleen and has the town on edge again." She made her shaky way across the room, dodging all the crap she leaves around her house. She sat in her chair and took a drink out of a glass that looked like it had been sitting there for days.

"If no one tells her anything, what can she do but go home?"

"She's not giving up, Helen. I told her I didn't know where her mother is, and that didn't work. Then I tried to explain what Colleen was like, and that didn't work either. She's going to keep digging and digging until she finds the right person to tell her about the night Colleen left."

I stand in the middle of the small room with my hands on my hips. "What's there to tell? She beat the crap out of me and left town."

"You were the last one to see her, Helen. If this girl gets the police involved, all of that will come out. Jonas and I can't protect you."

"What are you talking about? I was unconscious when you found me. How could I have done anything to her?" Anger curls in my stomach and begs to come out. I hated my sister for everything she put me through. And I wonder why Alice is bringing all this up now. Is she afraid of Natalie ?

"There was no police involvement that night. Jonas and I cleaned up the café. Sometime between when we got there, and he took you home, Colleen disappeared. We don't know what happened to her."

"You think I killed my sister?" I can't believe what I'm hearing. This woman has gone mad. "How could you think that? I was unconscious from the shovel she plowed into my head. Is that what Jonas thinks, too?"

Alice looks up at me through her coke bottle lenses. "You'll have to ask Jonas that. All I know is if the police are called, we have to tell them what we saw that night."

My hands shake. I want to grab the old woman out of her chair and shake her until she can't see straight. "You're going to tell the police that I killed my sister?" I ask my voice deadly quiet.

"If they ask, I'll have to tell them the truth, Helen. That's why we need to convince Natalie to leave before all this comes out again."

After all my family did for this woman, she's going to tell the police that I was the last one to see Colleen alive. And everyone in this town knows how I felt about my sister.

"I don't know what Natalie 's going to do, but I will talk to Jonas and get this straightened out." I storm to the door and open it.

"You'd better get Natalie to back off. If Colleen is dead, the police will come looking for you."

"I'll see you in hell first, Alice Perkins." I rush out and grab my bike. From the corner of my eye I see Natalie . She yells at me to stop, but I ignore her and take off down the sidewalk heading for Jonas's office building.

Now, back at my café, I walk in and everyone is standing next to the window looking at the hotel burning.

"Everything okay?" My front counter person, Lindsey, asks me. She's looking at me like I've suddenly sprouted two heads and a nose the size of China.

"Looks like quite a fire at the hotel. I sure hope they got everyone out of there." I purposely don't answer her personal question. No, everything isn't okay. I have a crazy woman threatening to tell the police that I killed my sister. And a girl who could be my sister's child, trying to find her when that's the last thing I want. Will everything ever be okay? I wonder as I walk back behind the counter and pour myself a glass of iced tea. Not if Natalie and Alice have their way.

Thirty years earlier

The pain pills my mother gave me finally took effect, and I fell asleep on the sofa with her hand stroking my hair. Sometime in the early hours of the morning, I awoke to my mother and father's voices, whispering in the kitchen.

"We found the sons of bitches. It's a good thing the sheriff got there first, or they'd be dead now for what they did to my baby."

Baby? Was he talking about me? He'd never called me anything but shithead my whole life. I stood up and crept closer to the kitchen. I wanted to hear what the sheriff said about Steve and Larry.

"Did he take them to jail?" my mother asked, like jail wasn't bad enough for those two.

"Yeah, he hauled them in. 'Course they were hollering all the way, saying Colleen lied; they didn't do nothing to her or Jose."

"Well, I'm glad they got them. I was afraid they'd let Larry go because of who his family is."

"I thought about that too, but the Sheriff is from Hood River, not here. Thank the good Lord."

"What happens next?"

I could hear my mother stirring around the kitchen, getting a drink from the faucet, and setting it on the table. I wanted to know what happened, so I scooted closer.

"They'll be arraigned in the morning. Colleen will probably have to testify at the trial."

"No!" Mama cried. "I don't want her to have to go through that."

"I'll be okay." I said, and they both turned towards me.

"What are you doing up, baby girl?" Mama hurried over and put her arm around me. "You should go back to bed. We can talk about this tomorrow."

Suddenly there was a loud knock at the door and my father got up to answer it. A sheriff's deputy was standing outside. I could see his uniform with the name Clint Andrews on it.

"I'm sorry, Mr. Winters, but the Sheriff called, and we have to take Miss Winters in for a rape kit. Should have done it as soon as she told us what happened, but with all that was going on, we forgot to mention it."

My father turned to me and for the first time ever, there was tenderness in his eyes. "I'm sorry, little girl, but we got to do it, or they won't be able to convict those SOB's."

Mama shook her head. "It won't do any good, deputy."

"Why not, Mrs. Winters?"

"Colleen came home and had a hot bath. I'm sorry, I didn't think." She held me close and there were tears in her eyes. "I should've known better."

The deputy stepped into the house. "Well, with Colleen's testimony, we can still get them on murder charges."

"Can't you go ahead and do the rape kit?" My father asked.

"We can, sir, but they are very expensive, and if it's inconclusive, it won't hold up in court."

I sagged against my mother. I knew that now was the time to tell them that I wasn't raped after all. But they couldn't prove otherwise, and if I kept my mouth shut, everyone in town would think it was true. I kept my mouth shut.

The deputy left soon after and Mama shuttled me back to bed. She lay down beside me, a protective arm around my waist. I couldn't sleep, and I knew she couldn't either. I laid there the rest of the night, crying over Jose and what I'd lost. Hate for Larry and Steve carved a black mark in my heart that I knew I'd never recover from.

The next few days passed in a dream. Larry and Steve were in jail without bail, waiting for their hearings. I wanted to see Jose's family, so my mother went with me. It was a warm day in June and the Santiago's had so many flowers growing in their yard, it was a riot of color. I looked at the tulips and daisy's and daffodils and realized that Jose was still alive when his parents planted them. Were the flowers a daily reminder of their loss? The cheerful blooms seemed almost garish up against the tragedy of losing Jose.

I knocked on the door and Jose's mother opened it. She was very pregnant, and I wondered if having another baby would help her get over losing her son. Somehow, I didn't think so. Her eyes looked old in a way that I had never seen on a woman her age before. When she saw me, she began to wail, her hands in the air over her head. Then she advanced on me, spewing words I couldn't understand because she was speaking Spanish, but I knew because of the tone of her voice, they weren't good.

"Eyee!" She cried, reaching out and shoving me hard. "No, no, no! You go away!"

I stumbled backwards, astonished at her anger towards me, and my mother was there, her arm firmly around me. "It isn't Colleen's fault, Mrs. Santiago."

"Eyee!" She cried again, holding her stomach and wailing.

Mama and I watched in horror as she folded into herself and fell to the floor, crying and speaking rapidly in Spanish, words that we didn't know.

Everardo came to the door and took his mother in his arms. "What's going on? *Mama, sigue adentro por favor.*" He gave us an anguished look.

"We wanted to pay our respects," my mother said, her voice soft with compassion. "We didn't mean to upset your mama."

"Please, leave us alone. You mean well, but you are a reminder to my parents of what we have lost."

We watched as he turned his mother towards the door of their house. Mama had her arm around me, and I was crying and shaking. My heart ached for their loss, and for mine.

I spent the summer mourning Jose and trying to work in the café. I stayed away from my friends. They tried to comfort me, but there wasn't anything anyone could do to make me feel better. Everyone in town was so kind. People I didn't know that well now knew who I was and stopped to say hello when they saw me. Even Helen was sweet to me that summer, which was very different than normal.

In September, I went back to school and that's when I did something I should never have done. I told my best friend, Patty West, that I wasn't raped.

"You weren't? But everyone in town thinks you were. You told the police you were." Patty had strawberry blonde hair and big grey eyes. Her skin was fair, and she had freckles across her nose.

We were sitting out by the river, talking. I watched a boat speed past. It was a warm fall Saturday and there were lots of people in the river on jet skis' and water skis. "The sheriff assumed I was, so I didn't correct him. They couldn't be tried for rape anyway. I took a hot bath and the rape kit wouldn't have found anything even if they had raped me. And they tried, Patty."

"I know. I'm sorry." Her eyes, a pale grey, flashed darker with her anger.

Later I wondered how long it was after Patty got home that she told her mother. And her mother told her best friend, and that friend told another and soon it was all over town that I lied.

CHAPTER 18: NATALIE

Present Day

I'm hunkered down between the toilet and bathtub, holding my breath, waiting for the next blast. After a few minutes I get up and grab a towel from the rack. If I don't get out of the hotel I'm going to die. I grab my bag and put my laptop in it. Then I soak the towel in water and put it over my face. Taking another towel, I put it over my hand and try the bathroom door which slammed shut in the blast.

To my surprise, the door opens. The room is thick with smoke. My eyes water and I can barely see, but it looks like the room is still okay. I hurry to the sliding glass door and yank on the handle. Tears stream from my eyes. I tug and tug on the door, then realize part of the glass has been broken out. I can get out. Thank God!

Another blast propels me forward and I feel something heavy drop on my foot. I glance down but it's too dark to see anything and I'm too concerned about getting out of the hotel to worry about my foot. I push through the broken glass and run full tilt into a fireman.

"Are you okay, miss?" He grabs my arm and hurries me

from the building. "We thought everyone was already out of there. Did you see anyone else?"

I think about the person who locked me in, but decide they are long gone. I hold my chest and cough until my eyes water and my stomach aches. "I don't think so."

We run from the building to the parking lot. There are people everywhere. The man who helped me assures himself that I'm fine and takes off. I'm standing watching the flames shoot up into the sky. My heart is racing, and my brain is numb. The popping and cracking of the fire, and the sizzle of the water hitting the hot building drown out the voices around me. Smoke swirls through the air and I have another coughing fit.

"Natalie! Thank God you're okay." Gayle Woods runs up and takes my arm. "I tried to stop you, but you just kept running. It's a wonder you got out of there alive."

If she only knew. I barely made it out with my life. I glance down at my bag and realize my laptop is gone. "My laptop. I had it in my bag."

Gayle looks at my bag. "Is that what you went back for? You can get another laptop. It's not worth your life."

I shake my head and reach into my pocket for the picture of my mother and it's not there. I burrow in my bag. Where did I put it? I thought I put it in my pocket. I search frantically through my bag. My heart dips and I get down on my knees, rummaging through my bag. I pull out my wallet, cosmetic case, notebook, and look through them, but still no picture.

I sink to the ground, feeling like I've lost her all over again. How many times am I going to lose my mother before I find her?

"What's the matter?" Gayle crouches down next to me.

"My mother. I had a picture of her. It must've fallen out

when I left my room." Tears blur my vision and I blink them away, looking towards the burning hotel.

Gayle takes my bag. "Is it okay if I look?

I nod, but I know it isn't there. I have a sinking feeling in my stomach that I've lost the picture.

Gayle goes through the bag. When she's finished, she shakes her head and hands it back to me. "I'm sorry."

"Me, too. That's the only picture I've ever seen of her." I swipe at the tears that are falling down my face.

"Maybe your room wasn't totally destroyed."

I nod, but looking at the fire, I'm afraid nothing could have survived. I'm lucky to have gotten out of there alive. I start shaking again and press my hand to my stomach.

Gayle stands up and reaches down to help me to my feet.

"Thank you. At least my car's still in the parking lot. I'm thankful for that. If all else fails, I may have to sleep in it tonight."

"They'll probably set up the school gym for people to stay, at least for a few nights," Gayle says. "That's what most towns do when things like this happen."

"Do you have a mayor?" I'm thinking that Cascade Locks is so small, there may not be a city government.

"Of course. My husband is the mayor." She looks around. "He's probably already trying to get things handled."

I think about what I still have. Luckily, I have my bag with me, and my driver's license and bank card are in there. I can rent another room if I have to. "I hope the hotel will refund the money for the rest of my stay."

"I'm sure they will. It may take a while though." She runs a hand through her short blonde hair. She's wearing sunglasses again and I wish she'd take them off, so I could see her expression.

"I wonder how it started."

Gayle shakes her head. "Who knows? Someone leaving a cigarette to near paper, or electrical wiring that went bad. I'm sure the fire department will find out and tell us."

"Hey honey, I've had to call a special meeting of the city council. I only have a few minutes before it starts. Would you go to The Sweet Onion and order food for us? The meeting will probably go through the lunch hour." Ben Woods walks up behind us and puts his hand on Gayle's arm.

Gayle jumps when he first starts talking, but she nods. "Sure. The usual?"

"That's fine. Have Helen send over a couple thermoses of coffee too. That should keep everyone happy for a while." He smiles at me and takes off for the hotel.

We watch him walk away, and then Gayle says, "I'd better go get lunch ordered for them." She touches my arm and starts to walk away. Then she turns back. "If you need anything, let me know, okay? And don't let this drive you away."

"I will, thanks." I watch her head for The Sweet Onion and wonder what she means by "don't let this drive you away?"

I walk closer to the hotel, wondering what will happen next. There are lots of people standing around wondering the same thing. "I left my purse in my room," one woman admits to me. She looks to be in her forties, tanned with bleached blonde hair and leathery skin that has seen a lot of sun. "All my identification and money's in it. I don't know what I'll do if my room is burnt."

We introduce ourselves and she tells me her name is, Holly.

"Hopefully, someone will tell us soon if our rooms are destroyed. Maybe we'll be able to salvage some of our stuff." My throat hurts from the smoke and I cough.

A woman walking by with a cooler filled with water bottles hands me one. "Here you go, honey."

I thank her and take a deep drink of the cold water letting it slide down my throat and soothe the soreness. Holly and I, along with several other people, stand around for what seems like hours watching the firemen trying to contain the fire. Finally, Holly suggests we go to the café and have a drink. We can see what's going on from there.

I'm ready to sit down, so I agree and walk to the café with her. "I need to call my husband," she says. "He didn't want me to come to Oregon alone, but I told him I'd be fine."

"And you are," I assure her.

"Yeah, but this is awful. I'll probably head home tomorrow." She digs her phone out of her bag.

"Are you here on business?"

She nods. "Yes, I'm a videographer. I'm here to film the Stern Wheeler Days for a magazine."

"It would be a shame for you to go home and miss it."

"I know, but I wonder if they'll even have the celebration now. A lot of people are going to have to get rooms in Hood River, if they can. When I was looking for a place to stay, I checked out Hood River and everything is full."

"Must be a popular place."

We order iced coffee and sit on the deck most of the afternoon. Holly tries to call her husband a couple times and finally gets hold of him. She moves off to talk in private and I sit and watch the activity in town.

My phone buzzes and I take it out of my bag. I don't recognize the number, but decide to answer it anyway, just in case it's someone from the hotel.

"Hello?"

"Natalie, it's Nick. I'm heading back from Stevenson and just heard about the fire. Are you okay?"

I'd forgotten I'd given him my phone number the day before. "Yes, I'm fine, but the hotel isn't. It's a mess, Nick."

"That's what I heard. Listen, if you need a place to stay tonight you can stay with Danny and me. We've got a spare bedroom. Danny said to tell you that he'd like that very much."

I smile for the first time in a while, thinking about Danny with his bright red hair and big grin. "That's so sweet of you both. I don't know what's going on yet. Can I let you know?"

"Of course. But from what I hear, they probably aren't going to let anyone back in the building for a while."

"Great. Well then, I may take you up on your offer."

Out of the corner of my eye, I see a person scurry up the road. At first, I think it's Alice Perkins, but by the time I turn around, whoever it is has disappeared.

Nick and I say goodbye, and I hang up, thinking about Alice. She couldn't walk that far, could she? I haven't seen her walk. I figured she had a hard time because she told me she did. Why would she be hanging out around the hotel? Maybe she's curious and came to look like hundreds of other people.

Word comes from a hotel employee that the school will be set up for people to spend the night there. They're offering food and a sleeping bag. I feel grateful that I won't have to sleep in a room with a hundred other people.

Nick shows up about a half hour later. I've moved from

the café back out on the sidewalk. He pulls up next to where I'm standing, and he and Danny get out.

"Wow!" Danny looks at the hotel with big eyes. "There's a lot of smoke."

"Yes, there is." I cough, and Nick asks if I want to sit in his pickup while he finds out what's going on.

"No, I'm fine." I cough again, covering my mouth with my hand and he gives me a worried look.

"Let me go talk to the fire chief. Maybe he'll give me some answers."

I nod, and Danny stays with me while he takes off.

"I'm glad you're going to stay with us." Danny puts his hand in mine. "Dad was really worried about you when we heard the hotel was burning."

A soft curl of warmth hits my mid-section, and I smile. We stand there watching the firemen work, then before I know it, Nick's back.

"I'm going to take you two to the house if that's okay, Natalie? There isn't anything we can do here, and you need to get out of this smoke."

"Okay, thank you. Are you sure you want a guest for the night?"

Nick smiles and my heart jumps in my chest. "I'm sure." The look he gives me causes chills to race up and down my arms. My last boyfriend, Jared, and I broke up over a year ago. We broke up because neither one of us was that invested in the relationship. I haven't dated anyone since. Not because I don't want to, I haven't found anyone I'm interested in. Until now. Until Nick. Oh heavens, this could be bad. I can't have a crush on Nick. I don't know who I'm related to in this town.

I follow him to the pickup and get in on the passenger side. Someone calls Nick's name and he stops to talk to a deputy. Danny's telling me they were planning to go to Portland for supplies Nick needs for a job. I'm looking in the backseat at him when Nick opens the door to the pickup.

He gets in and smiles at me, a smile that hits me in the gut and curls my toes. What is with this? I've got to stop being so attracted to him. I don't even know the man. I give him what I hope is a friendly, but not too friendly smile in return. I'm pretty sure I'm not too successful about keeping a distance between us when his smile turns into a grin.

Nick starts the pickup and makes a U turn in the road. "What a mess. They've called the Sheriff's office in because they're pretty sure it's arson."

"How did they find that out so fast?"

"What's arson?" Danny asks from the backseat.

Nick looks at him through the rearview mirror. "It's when someone deliberately sets a fire." He turns back to me. "They're pretty sure it was started in one of the guest rooms."

"Why would anyone start a fire in a hotel? Unless..." I stop talking and Nick glances over at me.

"Unless?"

"Nick, what if it's another warning? What if whoever left the warning message is behind this? I should've listened to you and called the Sheriff yesterday." I sit back against the pickup seat feeling guilty for not letting the Sheriff know what's going on.

"It's not your fault, Natalie. We don't know that it was the same person, and even if it is, how could you know this would happen?"

"I didn't, but I had a call last night."

"A call? From who?"

"I don't know. The phone in the room rang and I

answered it, and no one was there. All my friends back home have my cell phone number. They wouldn't call the hotel, and I don't know anyone here who would either."

"I really don't like this." Nick shakes his head and pulls into the driveway of a two-story grey house. The door is a dark brown wood and the windows are trimmed in white.

"This is beautiful. Did you build it?"

Nick looks at the house in front of us and nods. "About five years ago. I'd worked for my dad's company for ten years before I decided to build a house for myself."

Danny bounds out of the pickup and hollers for me to join him. "Come on, Natalie. I'll show you around."

Nick smiles. "Go take the grand tour while I get us a cool drink." He walks to the front door with me and opens it with a key on his key ring.

The inside is cool, and I close my eyes for a minute to enjoy the air conditioning. Then they snap open of their own accord. What have I done? Have I brought destruction on this small town? Nausea hits me with a force that almost takes me to my knees.

CHAPTER 19: HELEN

Present Day

After we close the café for the night, I drive out to Jonas' house. He lives on the eastern edge of Cascade Locks in what most people in this town might think is a mansion. His family built the massive wood and stone structure back in the thirties when they came to Cascade Locks from Oklahoma.

It's very ostentatious, I think as I drive up the long driveway and park in front of the three-story structure. At one time I hoped to live here someday as Jonas' wife. I had dreams of what we could do to the house and grounds, of our family---two girls and a boy---playing in the big yard and riding their bikes on the long driveway. But that didn't happen. Colleen made sure of that. After she left, I couldn't look at Jonas for a long time. I dated other men and Jonas stayed away from me.

I look up at the massive stone chimney that adorns one end of the house, and the plate glass windows that let light in year around. Someone has to clean all those windows, and I don't want to be the one to do that. Of course, I'm sure

Jonas has a cleaning team that comes in every week. He certainly doesn't have time.

I park my car and walk up to the front door, pushing the doorbell. It rings throughout the house. I wait for him to come to the door, but he doesn't come, so I push the bell again. When he still doesn't answer, I walk around back. Maybe he's in the pool.

The backyard is landscaped like a park, with flowers and bushes and bark dust scattered around. The pool house door is open, but I don't see Jonas. I walk towards the pool house, thinking he's in there for some reason.

"Jonas?" I stick my head inside and look around. Jonas is sitting on a bench with an old wooden chest at his feet. It looks like he's reading a letter. He jumps when he hears my voice.

"Helen? What are you doing here?" He thrusts the letter inside and closes it with a snap.

I walk further into the cool building. "I need to talk to you. I've been trying to find you all day."

He pushes the chest under the bench with his foot. "Well, now you've found me. Let's go back to the house. I have a bottle of Rose' chilling. Have you eaten? I bought a couple steaks to grill."

I stare at his face, searching for answers to what's in the letters he's reading. His cheeks are flushed, and I wonder what's so personal that he doesn't want me to know what's in them. "Sure. What can I do to help?"

"You can make a salad if you like." Jonas closes the door of the pool house as we leave, and we walk to the back entrance of his home.

"I thought you might be in the pool."

He gives me a brief smile, and I realize we are being

careful with each other. Something has changed between us, but I'm not sure what.

"I thought about it when I got home from work. We were up in Lyle today working on the Carter house. It's hot out there."

"Why were you working? Don't you usually leave it to the carpenters and sub-contractors?" I'm talking to him, but my mind is still on the wooden chest in the pool house. What was in it that captivated his attention?

Jonas leads me into the kitchen. Everything about this house is huge, over-powering, much like Jonas himself. The kitchen has a large cooking area, a table that seats twenty people and a fireplace with two easy chairs. "Yes, but this is the Carters, and they expect me to be involved. It's a three-million-dollar house. For that kind of money, I want to oversee every aspect of the building of it."

I can't fault him for that. He built his reputation by building high-end homes. "You'll have to take me over to see it someday."

He nods and takes the salad fixings out of the refrigerator and puts them on the counter. "If you want to start the salad, I'll turn on the grill."

He goes back outside, and I grab a knife from the knife block on the counter and start to chop the radishes and mushrooms. Jonas is organized. He cleans his vegetables before he puts them in the fridge, so it's easy to make a salad when he's ready. I have to be organized at the café. Home is another story.

When the steaks are grilled to perfection and the salad made, we sit at the table to eat. Jonas pours us each a glass of wine. I take a drink and realize this is what I needed today.

"So, what did you want to talk to me about?" Jonas cuts a bite of his steak and pops it in his mouth.

I'm not sure how to begin, so like always, I lay it out for him. "I'm worried about Alice."

"Alice Perkins? Why?"

"She threatened me."

Jonas puts his fork down and stares at me. "Why would she do that?"

"Jonas, she's very unnerved by Natalie being here. I don't know what's up with her, but she told me that if Natalie stirs things up about Colleen and the Sheriff starts asking questions, that you and she can't confirm that I was unconscious when Colleen left town."

"That's crazy. That was twenty years ago. Why would the Sheriff worry about Colleen now?" Jonas takes a big swig of wine and I notice that his hands are gripping the glass so hard it may shatter.

"I don't know. But Alice is acting like something bad happened to Colleen. Why would she think that? Didn't you see her before she left town?"

Jonas's grip on the glass tightens and I hold my breath that he won't drop it or squeeze so hard it breaks. He chews on his food for a minute, not answering me. A frown deepens the lines around his mouth. I find myself not breathing, waiting for his answer. "Yeah, she was a mess, but she didn't say much. I wasn't really in the mood to talk anyway. You were lying there, not moving, and I was terrified she'd killed you."

"So, she took off?"

"Yes, she and Alice were arguing when I got there. I told Alice I was going to take you to the hospital, but you came around and I knew you were okay. I brought you here instead. Alice cleaned up around the café, and then she and Colleen took off." He sets the glass down and I breathe a sigh of relief.

The salad dressing is sitting on the table between us, and I pick it up and pour more on my salad. Then I take a bite. "So, she was the last one to see Colleen?"

Jonas puts his knife down and shakes his head. "That's what she said. Now it sounds like she's changing her story. She's getting old. Maybe she's getting forgetful. She spends a lot of time alone."

"I hadn't thought of that, but now that you mention it, she does act like she's not quite with it anymore. She sits in that filthy house and lets the ladies from the church feed her. She never leaves the house, which is enough to make you loony. I'm surprised the church ladies haven't gone in and given it a good cleaning."

"She's let it go that much?"

"Yes, you should see it. It's horrible. It's like she's lost the will to live since Steve died."

Jonas looks worried. "I just heard about that. He was due to get out of prison, wasn't he?"

I nod. "He was murdered by an inmate." I eat a couple bites of my steak. "You know she never was the same after her son was sent to prison for killing that Mexican boy."

Jonas drains his wine glass and gets up to refill his and mine. "No, she wasn't. That was a tough time for her. And then Larry got out a few years ago on good behavior, but Steve didn't, and I think that did something to her too."

"Where's Larry? I thought he'd come back to Cascade Locks, but he hasn't."

"No." Jonas gets a faraway look in his eyes. "He doesn't want anything to do with this town. He moved to Portland after he left the half-way house."

"Do you ever see him?"

Jonas shakes his head. "He only calls when he needs

money. Our parents left him a trust fund, but I have control of it. And that makes him angry as you can imagine."

"Yeah, it would be hard to have to ask your brother for money all the time. Why do you suppose they set it up that way?"

"They were so heartsick when it came out that he and Steve murdered that boy. They didn't think they could trust him with a large amount of money, but they wanted him to have something when he finally got out of jail. At the time, I assumed they'd be alive when he got out, but that didn't happen."

"Your brother and my sister really messed up their lives." I finish my food and put my fork down.

"Yes, they did. And they tried to mess up ours."

"Actually, they did ruin ours. Don't you think that if they'd been more normal, we'd have had a more normal life?"

Jonas sits back and looks at me. "After all these years, I think it's time to stop letting them ruin us." He takes my hand, running his fingers lightly over my palm. "Helen, marry me."

I stare at him, not knowing whether to laugh or cry, so I do both. "You...what? You're asking me to marry you?"

"Don't you think it's time? We've danced around this subject for thirty years. I had planned to propose, and then Larry and Steve killed that kid and went to prison. By the time I got my head back on, you were engaged to Bonner. Then I married Donna and had Nick, and that didn't work because I still loved you."

Tears are falling down my cheeks in torrents. "You... love...me?" He'd finally said the words I'd waited so long to hear. I should be ecstatic, but there was something wrong with this proposal. Maybe it's because it came so late in our story. Or maybe he's proposing for some other reason, like he wants to distract me from something else. I look at this man that I know so well and see that he doesn't want to look me in the eyes. He's trying to be romantic, holding my hand, caressing it. But his mind is a million miles away.

Present Day

"Come on, Natalie. I'll show you my bedroom." Danny grabs my hand and drags me to the stairway next to the living room.

I shake off my guilt and follow him. Upstairs there are three bedrooms, a bathroom and an office. Danny runs through each room, anxious to show me his space. When I walk in the door, I notice the typical little boy decorations. There's a twin bed with a Star Wars comforter. There are shelves with every Star Wars toy you can imagine. A bookcase is overflowing with books.

"This is great, Danny. Did you pick out your comforter?"

"Yeah, me and Dad. We like Star Wars. We've watched all the movies a zillion times." He grabs a light saber and swishes it around the room.

Nick sticks his head in the door. "How about Polish dogs and French fries for dinner?"

"Yes!" Danny pumps his fist in the air.

"That work for you, Natalie?" Nick smiles at Danny's enthusiasm.

"Sounds wonderful. What can I do to help?"

"If you've finished your tour, come and talk to me. I'll pour us a glass of wine."

I head for the door. "That sounds heavenly. But let me do something to help."

Nick shakes his head. Then he turns to his son. "Danny, why don't you grab a shower?"

"Ah Dad, do I have to?"

"Yup." Nick looks at the silver watch on his wrist. It has a dark blue face and a wide silver link band. "It's getting late, buddy. You need to hit the sack."

"Okay." Danny heads to his dresser and pulls out clean pajamas.

Nick smiles and holds the door so I can go back downstairs with him.

Dinner is as good as if we have a gourmet meal. After he eats, Danny starts to fade and Nick packs him off to bed. Then we sit out on the patio and talk late into the night. Nick tells me a little about Danny's mother and how her illness affected their lives.

"Danny's had a hard time adjusting." Nick's voice is soft in the dim light.

The darkness brings with it an intimacy that wouldn't normally be there between two people who don't know each other any better than Nick and I do. "I'm sure. Poor little guy. But he tells me that you are a great dad."

Nick laughs. "I try. I wasn't expecting to be thrust into fatherhood, especially so soon after Liz and I got married, but I'm glad she felt like she could leave him with me."

"There wasn't anyone else? No family who would take him in?"

"No, her mom is a drunk who deals cards in an Indian casino. And her sisters are single moms who don't need more kids to take care of."

I turn towards him. "You must've been shocked when she asked you to adopt him."

"Yeah, we had only been married a couple months when she found out she had cancer. She was devastated, not knowing what would happen to Danny if something happened to her. The cancer was all over her by the time they discovered it. When she asked me to keep him, I didn't know what to say." He shakes his head at the memory. "My first thought was, I can't be a dad to a little guy I hardly know. And what do I know about being a father anyway."

I'm blown away by this man. Who takes a child to raise that doesn't belong to them? I stop short at that thought because that is exactly what Leona did. But why did she do it? I've been asking myself that ever since I found out she lied to me.

The next morning Danny wakes me up early. I shower and wash my hair with Nick's shampoo, and then when I get out, I pull it back into a ponytail.

I meet Nick in the kitchen where he's fixing breakfast. "What would you like to eat? We have cantaloupe, cereal, eggs, bacon, and toast, whatever you prefer." He gives me a smile that makes my heart do flip flops.

"Toast and cantaloupe sound good." I walk over and begin cutting up the cantaloupe, not wanting him to wait on me again.

After breakfast, we clean up the kitchen and then Nick says he needs to make some business calls, so Danny and I go out for a walk.

The day is just beginning. The sun is coming up over

the hills, brightening the sky and warming the air. I know it's going to get hot later, but for now, it's perfect. I take a deep breath and inhale the fragrance of the honeysuckle next to Nick's house.

Danny takes my hand. "Sometimes there are wild bunnies on the edge of the lawn. Let's see if we can find them." He puts his finger to his lips. "We have to be quiet." We walk around the yard, not talking and not spotting any bunnies either. Then Danny spots a bird's nest and points to it. "Look, Natalie."

I smile at the baby birds with their mouths open, waiting for mama to come fill them.

Nick calls for us and we head back to the house. As we walk in the door he says, "Natalie." Something in his voice sends terror through me and I turn to look at him. "Yes?"

There's another man standing next to Nick in the kitchen. He's wearing a uniform and my stomach drops. "This is Deputy Gardner. He needs to talk to you."

I look at the man standing next to Nick. "Deputy?"

He plays with his hat, turning it over and over in his hands. "Ms Merin, I'm sorry, but you're going to have to come with me. The sheriff wants to talk to you."

"What's wrong?" I look from him to the grim look on Nick's face. I'm getting a sinking feeling inside.

"You were staying in room number three at the Best Western Hotel?"

"Yes." I don't know where this is going, but he's so serious, I know it isn't going to be good. My insides clench and I feel guilty even though I know I haven't done anything wrong.

"It looks like that's where the fire started, Ms Merin. The hotel staff said they smelled smoke and went to check, and room number 3 had smoke coming out from under the door."

"You're kidding! And you think I did it? I wasn't even there. I went to Nick's office to talk to his dad. You can ask the receptionist."

He nods. "We will, ma'am, but the Sheriff wants to talk to you first. Why would someone start a fire in your room?"

"I have no clue why anyone would start a fire in my hotel room." What do they think I have in there? I think about the message telling me to leave and stop asking questions, and I realize that I am making somebody very unhappy by looking for Colleen Winters. Who? I wonder as I start to follow the deputy to his car.

"I'll go with you," Nick says, looking back at Danny, then at me.

"No, Nick, I'll be fine." I think about Danny's adventuresome spirit and how he almost fell off the cliff yesterday. "You need to stay with Danny."

Nick agrees and watches us walk away. I give him a smile that he returns, but I can tell he's worried about me.

It doesn't take us long to drive to City Hall where the Sheriff has set up a makeshift office. We park in the street and walk to the front door. It's starting to get hot. The deputy wipes his forehead against the shoulder of his uniform.

I look around and the street is already busy. The fire has been put out and all but one of the fire trucks has left the parking lot of the hotel. Sheriff's deputies are trying to get people to move off the street so they can have at least one lane open, but they are crowding the restaurant and the Sweet Onion café.

It's cool inside City Hall. The building is old and built well, and I'm sure it stays cool inside, even on very hot days.

The Sheriff has set up a temporary office in one of the rooms near the entrance. "Sheriff, this is Ms Merin." The deputy who walked over with me greets the man sitting behind a large wooden desk. The desk is old and scared from too many years of use. There are names carved into the flat surface.

"Ms Merin." The Sheriff stands up and holds out his hand. "Grant Anderson."

"Please call me Natalie." I shake hands with him.

He thanks me and indicates the chair across from him. "Have a seat. Would you like a cup of coffee?"

I notice there's a cup of coffee in front of him, but I shake my head and sit on the hard wood chair and look at him. He's an older man, probably in his early sixties, with short grey hair and a slightly darker mustache. He's tall and slender and reminds me of someone, but I can't figure out whom. Maybe a teacher I had in school.

He shuffles several papers in front of him. "So, I wondered if you could shed light on what's going on at the hotel."

"Not really." I lay my hands in my lap and try to relax. After all, I'm not on trial, so why are my hands sweating? "I heard the fire was started in my room, but I didn't start it. I wasn't even there when it started, besides, why would I?"

He gives me a hard look. "That's a good question. Why would you?" He looks at me over the top of his glasses. "I'm told you are here trying to find your birth mother. Is that correct?"

"Yes." I wonder why that has anything to do with the fire.

"And that you've been stirring things up around town, asking questions."

"Excuse me? Stirring things up? I've been asking if

anyone knows her. I don't think that's stirring things up." I think about the picture I'm sure has burnt up in the fire and my heart sinks. I want that picture. It's the only link to my mother that I have.

"Tell me what you know about her."

I tell him everything I've learned so far. That she lived in Cascade Locks twenty years earlier and disappeared one day. That she wasn't well liked, and that her sister hated her.

"You haven't any idea what happened to her?"

I shrug. "Not really. There are rumors going around that she was murdered, but I don't know how reliable they are. There are also rumors that she left with some guy and went to California. Apparently, she really liked men." I find myself hating to talk about her this way. What if it's only rumors and she was a good person? I don't want to malign her character. After all, I am a product of her, even if it's only in some small way.

"I heard you were threatened."

Suddenly the chair feels harder. "Someone left a note in my room. I still have....oh, no I don't." For a second, I forgot that my room had burned and everything with it. The sheriff is already acting like he doesn't believe me and now I have no proof.

"What did it say?"

"It said, Stop asking questions. Go home!"

He takes off his glasses, which were resting on the end of his nose, and rubs his eyes. "And you don't have any idea why this person would want you to stop asking questions about your birth mother?"

"No, I wish I did."

"And you have no idea who would start a fire in your room at the hotel?"

"No. I didn't have any secrets stashed away in there. Just the things I brought with me." Like my mother's picture.

"Has anything else happened since you arrived in Cascade Locks?"

"Like what?"

He shrugs and gives me a direct look. I tell him about the late-night phone call, and he mutters something about how it may have been a wrong number. I don't believe that for a second. If it was a wrong number why did I hear breathing on the other end?

"Okay." The sheriff stands, so I do, too. "Thanks for coming over to talk to me. If you get any more threats or remember something that would help us find out who started this fire, please let me or one of my deputies know."

"I will." I have a bad feeling about this. The sheriff acts like he thinks I came to Cascade Locks to cause trouble and started the fire for some crazy reason that makes no sense.

"Oh, and Ms Merin?"

I turn back to look at him.

"We will be keeping an eye on you while you're here."

Nick and Danny are waiting outside in Nick's pickup when I get through. "You didn't have to come get me," I tell Nick. My heart is pounding from the sheriff's last words. I just want to get in my car and drive as far from here as I can get.

"We wanted to," Danny chimes in from the backseat.

I smile at him and climb in the passenger side where Nick is holding the door open. "Don't you need to get to work?"

"Not for a while. Let's go back to my place where we can talk." He shuts the door and rounds the pickup and gets in on the drivers' side.

Danny has brought two of his Star Wars figures and is engaged in a battle in the back seat.

"How did it go?" Nick drives down the street until he can turn around and head back to his house.

"I'm not sure. He acted like I deliberately started that fire. Why would he think that?"

"He's gathering information. I doubt he thinks you started it."

"I don't know. He sure acted like it. And he told me that they're going to be watching me while I'm here."

Nick chuckles. "Not sure how they'll do that. They are hardly ever here. A deputy cruises through occasionally, but there isn't a police force here."

"Sheriff Anderson seemed very interested in what I know about Colleen." The passenger side window is down, and the wind is blowing my hair all over my face. I scrape it back and hold it away from my eyes. "He kept asking me questions about my search for her. That seemed strange to me."

Nick takes his eyes off the road and glances at me. Concern darkens his face. "That is strange." He's quiet for a few minutes. "How old is Colleen?"

"I don't know. I think she had me when she was nineteen, and I'm twenty-eight, so she'd be...forty-seven?"

Nick nods. "I'm pretty sure Sheriff Anderson used to live in Cascade Locks. He was a deputy sheriff for a while, then about fifteen years ago he ran for Sheriff and he's held that position since. I wonder if he was here when Colleen was still around."

"Maybe. What are you thinking?"

He shrugs. "It's just a hunch, but let's do an online search on him and see if we can find out anything. Maybe he knew your mother."

My stomach dips. "Maybe he was here when she went missing?"

"He might have been." He turns on the blinkers and pulls into his driveway. "If he was, it might be interesting to know what he knows."

"And why he didn't volunteer that he knew her." I put my hand against my stomach, feeling it flutter.

Nick puts the truck in park and turns off the engine and we jump out and hurry to the house. We're almost there when Danny runs up behind us. "What's the hurry? You need to go to the bathroom?"

Thirty years earlier

A couple of days after I told Patty my secret, I was working at the café, bussing tables when a woman walked in. She was dressed nicely in black slacks and a red sweater and had her hair done by the beautician in town. I could tell because it looked like every other woman in town's hair. I'd seen her around and knew she was Lynn Holden, a friend of Carol White, Larry's mother. My first thought when I saw her was, this wasn't going to be good.

She walked up to me and stuck her finger in my face. Without thinking, I backed up and found myself against the counter. Her breath smelled like coffee and cigarettes with a hint of garlic. My stomach churned. Her lips barely moved when she said, "you should be ashamed of yourself. How dare you put the White family through this? I knew you were lying. I told my husband that you are a liar and he didn't believe me."

My hands started to shake. I didn't know what to say to her. "I...I..."

"Don't go making excuses. You've put that poor Larry

through hell for no reason. You've been sleeping with that Mexican boy. You're probably the one who killed him. You or that drunken father of yours. I hope the devil comes tonight and takes you both." With that, she stormed out of the café.

Tears spurted from my eyes. I sat down at a table and put my head in my hands. I was so glad that my Mama hadn't heard this. How could she say such vile things to me? She didn't know what I went through, or how much I miss Jose, and feel guilty about his murder, or how awful it was to have that nasty Steve's hands all over me. I remember the nausea that overwhelmed me when he was mauling me. It returned, and I held my stomach, afraid I was going to puke.

The door opened, and I kept my head down. Mama hadn't been feeling well and wasn't going to come in today. As much as I wanted her to feel better, I hoped wasn't her. I didn't want her to see me like this. I stood and staggered to the door. A soft hand reached out and stopped me. "What's the matter, honey?"

Leona was a nurse at the hospital, but she worked part time for Mama cooking at the café. She had always been nice to me, but I wondered how she'd act when she found out what I did.

I shook my head and tried to move past her. She reached out and gathered me into her arms. "Tell me what happened." Her voice was soft and calm, and I found myself blurting out what I did and how Lynn accused me of killing Jose.

Leona was tall and slim, but as she pulled me into her embrace, I felt comforted. She smoothed my hair back from my face. "Don't listen to what people say, Colleen. If you do, you'll always be upset. Those boys killed Jose and tried to rape you. They deserve to be punished."

"But I did lie about the rape."

She nodded. "And you need to tell the truth about that, but what you did isn't even close to what they did to you."

I swiped at the tears and gave her a hug. "Thank you."

She hugged me back. "No need for thanks. Now go wash your face. You can't take care of customers with mascara running down your cheeks."

I did what she said and felt better. When I went back into the café, there were people I knew sitting at a table. I walked over to take their orders and they got up without saying anything and walked out.

Leona's face was set in a grim mask. She shook her head and handed me a clean wet cloth. "Why don't you wipe down all the tables."

The rest of the day was busy. Most people gave me surprised looks, but they didn't say anything. I was relieved that they didn't stomp out because I was there. Mama needed their business. She called and asked how things were going and I told her everything was fine.

Around closing time, Larry's mom, Carol White walked in. My heart sank. Leona came from behind the counter and stood next to me.

"Is it true?" Carol asked me. "Did you lie about Larry raping you?" Her eyes were the color of steel. She leaned towards me and Leona put her arm around me.

"It wasn't Larry," I whispered. "He didn't touch me. He just threatened to. Steve tried to rape me, but I got away."

"Why did you lie?" Carol had big shoulders and she was taller than my dad. She towered over Leona and me, her eyes boring into me.

"They weren't charged with rape." My voice came out small and shaky which really made me mad. Why should I be afraid of what this woman said?

"No, but you let everyone think you were raped." Her narrowed eyes bore into me.

Leona held up her hand. "I know you're upset, but the evidence proved that your son and Steve Perkins killed Jose. Colleen should've told the truth about the rape, but she was traumatized by them and Jose's murder. She's going to tell the sheriff the truth now, aren't you, Colleen?"

She looked at me and I nodded.

"Lot of good that will do." Carol took my arm and squeezed so hard I knew I'd have a huge bruise there. "There will be people who believe her even if she is a lying little tramp." She let go and stormed towards the door.

I was glad she was leaving and started to pull away from Leona, but Mrs. White stopped at the café door and looked back. Her eyes were slits in a white face, and her voice was full of evil. "You tell your mom she needs to find a job somewhere. If I have anything to say about it, no one in this town will ever step foot in this café again."

CHAPTER 22: NATALIE

Present Day

Nick and I are leaning over his desk searching the internet for anything on Grant Anderson. Nick's fingers fly across the keyboard. Danny has given up on us and gone to play with the neighbor boy. I scoot a chair up next to Nick's desk and read the articles he's bringing up on the sheriff.

Nick sighs and shakes his head. "He's in the Hood River News a lot which is normal since he's the sheriff of Hood River County. But I can't find anything about where he lived twenty years ago."

"Maybe we should ask him."

Nick chuckles and leans back in his chair and rubs his eyes with his hand. "Might be easier. I'm not sure what we thought we'd find anyway, but I can keep looking." He gets up and walks to the window. His office looks out on the backyard where Danny and his friend are kicking a ball around. Nick smiles at their antics.

I watch them for a couple minutes, and then turn back to the computer. "Hey, they've got an article on the fire already."

"I'm not surprised. There were News vans everywhere. It was probably on TV too." Nick leans over my shoulder and reads the article I'm reading. "Not much we didn't already know."

I finish reading the article. "The fire department did a great job putting the fire out so quickly. I'm glad that was mentioned."

"Yeah, we have a good team here for such a small place. They're all volunteers."

I go back to the newspaper achieves to see if I can find out more about Sheriff Anderson, but I can't find anything that ties him to Cascade Locks or to Colleen. "You'd think there would have been an article about Colleen's disappearance."

"You'd think, but it sounds like they thought she left on her own, so why would it be in the news?"

I'm so sure by now that she didn't leave of her own accord, that something did happen to make her leave, or that she was murdered. I'm starting to think she may have been murdered, and I don't want to go there.

"I can ask my dad. He's been acting squirrelly lately, but he would know if Anderson was around back then. I'll call him."

While Nick makes the call, I walk around the room looking at pictures of him and Danny at different vacation spots. There's one of Danny taken with one of the Disney characters. He looks about three years old. Another is of the two of them at a Hawaiian luau. Another shows them riding horses on a beach.

Behind me I can hear Nick talking to his father. "I was just curious. He's in town looking into the fire at the hotel."

I walk back over to the computer and do a search on

missing women in the area back in two thousand and six. Several names show up, but not Colleen's. Then I add Sheriff Anderson and an article in the Hood River News pops up. I make a small sound in my throat.

Nick says thanks and goodbye to his dad and scoots his chair closer to me. "What did you find?"

I point to the computer screen. An article in the May 15, 1988 edition shows a picture of Anderson and another man. The title reads, "Local deputy finds the body of a Cascade Locks man."

The remains of a young man from Cascade Locks were found yesterday near the trail head of the Pacific Crest Trail. Deputy Grant Anderson says a tip from an anonymous source led the Sheriffs' department to the area west of the trail where they found the body of Jose Santiago, a Mexican native, who has been living in Cascade Locks with his family for the past three years. The investigation is pending, but the Sheriff's office is suspecting foul play.

A young woman, whose name has not been released, claims that she knows who killed Mr. Santiago. The Sheriff has stated that they are looking into her claims.

"Is that the only article? Keep looking, there has to be more." Nick is sitting close to me and I can feel the heat from his body. There's an electrical current running from him to me, charging my nerve ends. My heart pounds and my throat is dry.

"That's all I found." I tell him. "You'd think there would be something in the next edition of the Hood River News, but there isn't."

"Huh. I asked my dad about Anderson and he said he used to live in Cascade Locks, but he moved to Hood River when he became Sheriff."

"So, he could have known Colleen."

Nick nods.

"I should have asked him about her. I don't know why I didn't." I'm regretting not thinking of asking him if he knew her.

"We can go over to the courthouse and try and see him again." He's continuing to search the Hood River News for anything else involving the sheriff and Cascade Locks. There are a few more articles, but we know it was around twenty years ago when Colleen disappeared, so our excitement over our search is fading.

Nick looks at his watch. "It's almost noon. Why don't I take you to Hood River to get what you need? We can have lunch while we're there."

"You don't have to do that. I've still got my rental car."

"Yes, but Danny needs jeans and Wal-Mart is the best place to find them around here. That kid is growing so fast it feels like I'm buying him new clothes every other week." He shakes his head. "Unless you'd rather go by yourself?"

"Of course not. I just don't want to keep you from whatever you were planning to do today."

Nick smiles. "I didn't have much going on. Planned to go into the office this afternoon, but there isn't anything pressing."

"Okay. That will be great if we can stop by the courthouse first."

He agrees and calls Danny from the window. Danny's excited when he learns we're going to Wal-Mart. "One of his favorite places," Nick says.

We all get in Nick's pickup and he drives back into town and stops at the courthouse. The Sheriff has gone to Hood River for a meeting and isn't available. The deputy is closing the makeshift office. "We're still investigating, but we'll do it from the sheriff's office. The State fire investigator is on his way here today." He looks at me. "He'll probably want to talk to you."

My heart sinks. I wish I knew something that could help them find out who set the fire, but I don't know anything.

We say goodbye and take off for Hood River. Our first stop once we hit town is Taco Bell, Danny's favorite restaurant. We go inside and order. While we're eating, I look around at what I can see of the town. "Is Hood River bigger than Cascade Locks?"

"It's about seven thousand people in the winter but it probably swells to fifteen thousand in the summer with all the tourists."

"You're right, that is bigger."

"Dad, we should take Natalie for a drive and show her around." Danny is trying to talk around a mouthful of food and Nick tells him to finish chewing and swallowing before he speaks.

"Would you like to drive into town and see what's here?"

"Sure." I take a bite of my taco and smile at Danny who is enjoying his by the look on his face.

We finish lunch and Nick heads towards the center of town. There are several banks and fast-food places plus other businesses on Cascade Avenue where Taco Bell and Wal-Mart are. Once we near town, there are older homes in all shapes and sizes.

"This is beautiful." I look around at the old houses with their well-maintained yards.

"It's a pretty little town, but you should see the valley. There are orchards and Mt. Hood to the south of here. It's a gorgeous place. We'll come back and look around more before you leave."

"I'd like that." I make a mental note to come back when I have my own car, so I can look around more. There are some interesting looking shops downtown.

"Can we take Natalie to Mount Hood? We can show her Timberline Lodge. There may even be snow." Danny leans over Nick's seat to talk to him.

"Maybe another day, big guy. Right now, we need to get her some clothes since hers all burned up in the fire. And you need jeans and socks."

We head back to Wal-Mart to buy what we need. Once inside, Nick and Danny start towards the children's clothes and I find the Women's. There's enough to get me by until I can shop downtown at some of the nicer stores. I'm looking forward to that and hoping I can afford to take some fun things home with me. Maybe I can find a baby store and buy something for Hannah's baby.

I'm looking at underwear when my cell phone rings. I don't recognize the number but take the call anyway and to my surprise it's Gayle Woods.

"How did you get my number?" I ask her.

"It pays to have your husband be the mayor. The sheriff gave it to Ben, and he gave it to me."

"Okay." I'm not sure I like the sheriff giving my number out.

"I wanted to offer you the use of our guest house. It's right next door to our home and it's fully furnished. I know you want to stay in Cascade Locks, and I think the hotel will be closed for a while. Most of the people who were staying there are trying to get rooms in either Hood River or across the river in Stevenson."

"That's really nice of you." I'm relieved that I won't have to impose on Nick any longer. As much as I love being with him and Danny, I don't want to wear out my welcome. "I'll be happy to pay you rent."

"Come look at it and we'll talk. We don't usually rent it out, but this is an unusual circumstance." She gives me the address and I tell her that I'm in Hood River with Nick and will go see her when I get back to Cascade Locks.

Not long after that Nick and Danny find me, and we pay for our purchases and head back out to Nick's truck. When we get in, I tell him about Gayle's call.

Nick is silent for a few minutes and I glance at him, wondering what he's thinking. He starts the pickup and pulls out of the parking lot. "You're kidding me. Gayle offered her guest house?"

"Yeah. Why? Do you think that's a bad idea?"

"I guess it will be okay. But Danny and I like having you stay with us."

I smile at him, feeling that draw again. Knowing I'd better stay somewhere else until I know if we're related or not. "I loved staying with you, but I don't want to impose. Gayle says their guest house is empty and I can pay them rent. That way I won't feel like such a mooch."

"Of course, she wants rent. And you aren't a mooch." Nick concentrates on driving and I hope I haven't offended him. He has been nicer to me than anyone in Cascade Locks. He reaches over and touches my hand. "I'm sure it'll be fine. Just keep an eye on Gayle. It's not like her to be helpful."

"What do you mean?"

Nick scratches his head. "Well, I hate to say this, but she's good at looking out for Gayle. Not so good about caring for others. Be careful, okay?"

I nod, and then I remember that she took food to Alice.

Alice seemed to take it for granted that she did. I tell Nick and he looks surprised.

"She did? I thought Ben did most of the cooking." He shrugs. "Maybe I've misjudged her." He's quiet for a couple minutes then he says, "Just be careful. I'm not sure I trust her."

Present Day

Nick drives me to my car, which is still in the parking lot of the Best Western hotel. I'm so relieved to see it sitting there untouched by the fire. The firemen have left, and the parking lot is mostly empty except for a few official vehicles.

I look at the fire blackened wing of the hotel and shiver, thinking about how it felt when I thought I was trapped inside during the fire. I might've been killed. My hands start to shake and Nick reaches over and puts his warm hand on mine.

"It looks so dark and desolate," I whisper.

Nick follows my gaze, a grim look on his face. "I hope they find whoever did this."

"Me, too. What if someone had been trapped inside?" Now I'm thinking about the children of families vacationing in Cascade Locks. My stomach twists. "What have I stirred up by coming here?"

Nick takes my hand. "You don't know that this is about your search, Natalie. It could have been bad electrical wiring or anything, even a random arsonist."

I give him a small smile, but I'm sure that I've stirred up a hornet's nest of some kind. After all, I did get the warning to leave. *What did you do to make someone hate you so much?* I silently ask Colleen.

Before I get out of the pickup I turn to Danny. "Thank you for letting me stay with you."

For once his mouth is turned down instead of the big smile he usually has. He leans back against the seat, his arms crossed over his little chest. "I want you to stay with us. Why do you have to stay somewhere else?"

Nick stirs, and I glance at him. He's looking straight ahead. I lean over the seat and take Danny's small hand in mine. "Maybe we can spend some time together while your dad's at work? I hear you're in need of a babysitter."

"Really!" Danny grins and claps his hands. "Can Natalie be my babysitter, Dad?"

Nick gives me a surprised look. "We need to find a sitter to replace Chloe, but until we do, maybe you could stay with Natalie if she wants you too." He turns to me. "Are you sure?"

"Of course, I'd love to spend time with Danny. He can show me around Cascade Locks. That will give you time to find the right babysitter." I get out and gather my shopping bags.

Nick follows me to help. "I feel like we're taking advantage of you. I'll find a babysitter as fast as I can."

"I'm going to be here for a couple weeks. It will be fun to have Danny with me while you're working."

Danny climbs out and gives me a hug. "Am I coming to see you today?"

"Not today." Nick helps me carry my bags to my rental car. "Natalie needs to check on the place where she'll be staying and make sure she likes it." He places the bags in the trunk after I've opened it. "If you don't like the looks of their guest house, you can stay with us. Our guest room is yours."

On impulse I reach out to give him a hug. His arms close around me and he holds me close for a little longer than I expected. When he lets me go, we're both a little breathless. I smile up at him and he gives me a slow sexy smile, his dark eyes intent on mine. "Call me after you meet with Gayle and let me know what you're going to do, okay?"

"I will."

We say goodbye, and I get into my hot rental car and push the button to power the windows down. I wave at them as they pull out of the parking lot, my heart racing because of the feel of Nick's arms around me. Why do I finally meet a guy who really gets under my skin and he lives far away from me and could be related. I feel like crying. It isn't fair.

Nick pointed out the road where Gayle lives as we drove into town, so I don't have any trouble finding her house. It's in a new housing development on the east end of town. I don't think I'm far from Nick's office.

There's a bright red Miata sitting in the driveway when I pull in. It looks like something Gayle would drive. I park and walk up to the front door and ring the bell.

The house is a tan split level with the garage on the left of the front entrance. Gayle comes to the door wearing white leggings and a lilac tunic. "Come in." She moves back to give me room to enter.

Her house is cool and sparkling clean. "What a beautiful home."

"Thank you. I have a cleaning lady who comes once a week. It's so nice to not have to worry about keeping it clean." She shows me the sunken living room.

Everything is decorated in soft warm tones. The cream-colored carpeting is thick, and I can tell it's expensive. There's a grand piano near the sliding doors onto a patio. Most people would have used the space for a dining room, but the piano fits perfectly.

The kitchen is towards the back and it's bright and sunny. The cupboards are all white and she's decorated with yellow and blue.

"The guest house is out back." She leads the way to the outside door, and I follow her to a patio that runs the length of the house. There's a small red building not fifty feet from her back door and this is where she takes me.

It looks like a gingerbread house with its white trim and dark red paint. There's a seating area out front which has lawn chairs and a small table. There are pots of mixed flowers with daisies, Gerber daisies, asters, and snap dragons. There are also two hanging baskets full of red geraniums.

"This is really cute, Gayle."

She opens the door to let me see the inside. Once I walk in, I know I want to stay. The house is tiny, but perfect for one person. And it's decorated in feminine pinks and whites like a cottage and smells of lemon oil. "It looks like something out of a magazine."

Gayle smiles. "I'm glad you like it. I had fun decorating it. At first, I thought I'd use it as a studio, but I haven't painted in years and probably won't go back to it. So, we turned it into a guest house."

I look around at the plump sofa with a pink throw on one end, the white chair with striped pink and blue pillows resting on it. Above the sofa is a painting of a white vase full of pink roses. "Did you paint this?" I ask, pointing to the painting.

She nods. "A long time ago."

"It's perfect. You are very talented." I look around. "Thank you for thinking of me."

"You're welcome. I told Ben we need to offer it to one of the hotel guests and you were the first person I thought of."

"How much are you thinking of for rent?" I'm sure I'll get a refund from the hotel, but I don't know when and even though I have some money saved, I don't want to spend it all on this trip.

"You don't have to pay us anything. Ben is the mayor and he thinks it's a good will gesture that will impress the town. Maybe they'll remember next election." She laughs.

"I want to pay something. I don't feel right staying here for free."

"You can take that up with Ben." She heads into the tiny kitchen. "Let me show you where everything is. I know you went shopping, but if you need anything, just let me know. There should be everything here you'll need for your stay except your personal belongings and food."

She shows me where to find everything in the kitchen and bathroom. The house is so small, I don't think I will have trouble finding anything, but she seems to get great enjoyment out of showing it off.

"We're grilling chicken tonight. You can have dinner with us. I won't take no for an answer. Ben is great with the grill and I've bought more than enough food for us." She smiles and looks around the room. "We'll eat about six, so get settled in and come over when you're ready. I'll make a pitcher of margaritas."

After she leaves, I feel sort of like I've been in the eye of a hurricane. I put my meager supplies away and realize I need to run out for a few things from the grocery store before it gets too late.

Before I do that, I need to make a phone call to the sheriff and see if he'll tell me what he knows about Colleen. I dial the number for the sheriff's office in Hood River, but it rings and rings. Promising myself to try again later, I end the call.

I call Nick and tell him I love the guest house. He asks me what time I want Danny the next day and we agree on eight o'clock so he can get some work done.

The drive back into town takes me all of five minutes. I haven't been in the grocery before and it's fun to see what all is there. Even though it's a small store, they are stocked with enough groceries to get me by for several days. I'm happy to see that they have fresh bread from a bakery, and I buy a loaf of honey wheat.

When I go back outside to my car, Helen is parking her bike next to the store. I watch her lean it up against the building. She looks up and sees me and turns her head away. I stuff my groceries into the trunk and hurry after her.

"Helen!"

She stops and turns to me. Today her face isn't quite as stony as it has been every other time I've tried to talk to her. "What?"

"I'd really like to talk to you about your sister." I wish I had the picture of Colleen so I could show it to her.

She sighs. "Colleen left here twenty years ago. I don't know where she is and to be brutally honest, I don't care. I'm sorry I can't help you."

My heart sinks. Can't or won't? "Why did she leave?"

A dark shadow passes over her face and for a moment I think she's going to turn and walk away like she has every other time I've approached her. "I don't know." She gives me a thoughtful look. "So, if you think Colleen is your birth mother, who is your father?"

This pulls me up short. I've spent so much time concentrating on finding Colleen, I haven't thought much about the man who fathered me. "I don't know. Do you?"

She shakes her head and takes her sunglasses off. A grimace of pain crosses her face and is gone in an instant. "No, but maybe you should look for him. Maybe if you find him, you'll find Colleen."

CHAPTER 24: NICK

Present Day

The first thing I did when I heard about the fire at the hotel was to call Natalie. As much as I think I should stay away from her, I can't seem to make myself.

I hate it that she's staying in Gayle Wood's guest house instead of being here with Danny and me, even though I know that it's the best thing for all of us. But I'm not in the best of moods when Danny and I finish supper and he heads for the shower. After having her here for one night, I don't know what to do with myself now that she's gone. Pathetic.

The office computer is still on and I go in and sit down in front of it wishing I could find Colleen. That would make points with Natalie. I research Cascade Locks twenty years ago and find nothing except a few news articles about the toll on the bridge and who ran for mayor that year.

I go back another five years, just for fun, and scan the news articles for that year. Danny comes in dragging his favorite stuffed toy, a brown puppy he's had since he was a baby. He still cuddles with it at night.

"Here Dad, hold Ralphie for me." He tosses the toy to me and I catch it and hold it up to look at. "He's getting pretty worn out, Danny. Don't you think we should put him away, so he doesn't come apart?"

Danny leans over my shoulder and looks at the dog. There's a thread coming loose on one of the seams and he reaches out to pull on it.

"Don't do that, he will come apart." By the time the words are out of my mouth, there's a long string coming from Ralphie and a wail from Danny.

"It's okay, son, I'll sew him up." I hug Danny and get up to find a needle and thread, sure that I have one somewhere. There's a drawer in the laundry room where I keep everything that I don't know what else to do with. Since I don't sew often, like in almost never, I don't know for sure what's there, but it seems like I saw a packet of needles and some brown thread there once when I was looking for a nail to hang a picture.

Danny follows me into the laundry, and I open the drawer, starting to paw through it only to have help from little fingers that keep getting in my way. "Hey, do you want me to look or not? I can't see anything with you standing in front of me."

"Sorry." He backs off a fraction of an inch.

I find the needles and hold them up in triumph. "Ah, here they are. I knew they were in here. Let's see if there's some thread too."

Danny holds the needle packet while I rummage for the thread. There are scissors, coupons, rulers, pens, papers, menus, and a myriad of other things hanging out in this drawer. "Maybe I should take a day off and clean this drawer."

"Nah, then we'd never have stuff when we need to find something."

"True words, my man." I rummage some more and finally come up with the thread. It has come partially unraveled and is wrapped around a piece of paper. I pull the paper off and realize it's a newspaper clipping. I hold it up to see what it is and why I've saved it.

My heart almost stops when I realize it's an obituary for Liz, Danny's mom. When she died, I was so heartsick I didn't want to deal with anything. When did I cut this out of the paper and put it in this drawer?

I stuff it into my jeans pocket, not wanting Danny to see it and get upset all over again. He's starting to read and loves to read everything from road signs to the back of trucks. I don't want him to see his Mom's name and freak out.

"Let's see if we can fix Ralphie." It's times like this I wish Danny's mom was still alive. Or my mom lived closer, or something. My mind flies to Natalie. I'm sure she'd know how to fix an important puppy.

Twenty minutes later I want to throw the stupid dog down and stomp on it. I promised myself when Danny came to live with me that I wouldn't use cuss in front of him, but I'm tempted...man, am I tempted. I can't get the stupid needle threaded.

Danny's leaning over my shoulder trying to help, which is no help. Finally, I give up. "Sorry, little guy, I can't get this stupid needle threaded. I'll have to find someone tomorrow who can get thread through that tiny hole."

"No, Dad, I need Ralphie fixed tonight. What if I roll over on him and he comes apart? Please Dad? Don't give up."

I look at him and think, seriously? You're going to make that big of a deal over this? But the tears forming in his eyes are my undoing and I take a deep breath and try again. This time, by some miracle, it works.

I do the best I can. My stitches aren't perfect, but Danny is thrilled that Ralphie is back together. He gives me a hug, yawns and heads off to bed. After he's kissed goodnight, wrestled with for a bit and says his prayers, I turn off the light and close his door.

Back downstairs I fix myself a cup of coffee and sit down on my recliner. The television remote is waiting for me. I start to reach for it, but something makes me take the obit from my pocket instead.

Elizabeth Edwards White, beloved wife of Nicolas White passed on from this life in her home with her family surrounding her.

My eyes skim the rest of the obituary. I'm thinking about how I need to put this somewhere, so Danny can have it when he grows up. Then a name jumps out at me. *Elizabeth is also survived by her aunt, Leona of Kissimmee, Florida.*

Natalie's last name is and she's from Kissimmee. Is this a coincidence, or by some odd freak show is she related to my dead wife, and to Danny? I try to remember if she told me her grandmother's name, but I can't.

I call her cell phone, but she doesn't answer so I leave a message for her to call me. Then I go up to the office and dig through old files that once belonged to Liz, hoping I can find something about her aunt.

I've kept all this stuff in case there is information in here that Danny needs some day. I riffle through the files, but I don't find anything on Liz's family except the news articles she kept on the sports activities she and her sisters were involved with in school.

My phone rings and seeing Natalie's name come up I

grab it from the desk. "Natalie, what did you tell me was your grandmother's name?"

"My grandmother? Do you mean the woman who raised me?"

"Yes." I know it's a long shot, but I have a feeling I'm right.

"Leona . Why do you need to know?"

"Because I just found a link between her and Danny."

"What? What kind of link?"

"Natalie, Leona was my wife's aunt."

There's silence on the other end of the phone for several minutes. I kick myself for not waiting and telling her face to face. I know she's angry at her grandmother and the way she kept the truth of her birth family from her.

"You're kidding me."

"No, afraid not. But listen, this is good. Maybe Liz's mother will know something about Leona and your adoption. Maybe she knows Colleen and can tell you where she is."

Thirty years ago

After a dry hot summer, at the end of September we had our first rainfall of the season. I hated to see fall coming because that meant winter wasn't far behind.

I was at school, watching the girls' basketball game and I could hear rain pounding on the roof. I could even hear the claps of thunder over the sounds of the girls screaming and the coaches' whistle.

Patty was playing, and I'd stayed after school to watch her. There had been a strange feeling in the air today. Before seventh period, I walked into Mrs. Henderson's class and a couple of girls were already there. They were whispering and shut up the minute I walked in, looking at me over their shoulders.

I was getting used to my popularity; so, at first, when I realized how everyone was going to stand behind me and support me after what happened with Steve and Larry and Jose, it was weird to find all the snobby girls wanted to hang out with me and be my friend.

I wandered over to talk to them, and they both gave me

strained smiles and suddenly had somewhere else they needed to be.

I found that odd, but it wasn't the only time it had happened that day. I finally asked Patty if she knew what was going on. "I'm getting a feeling that I did something wrong, but I don't know what it is. Is something going on?"

We were at lunch and Carla and Joyce walked right by us and sat at a different table, even though I motioned for them to join us.

Patty's face turned bright red. "I don't know of anything."

I shrugged and let it go, but then it happened again at the basketball game when a couple of the girls wouldn't sit by me even though I saved seats for them.

My feelings were hurt, so I walked over and sat down next to Jason Daniels and Todd Wells. Carla has had a crush on Jason for ages and she shot daggers at me with her eyes from across the room.

Jason and Todd seemed happy to have me with them and we talked and laughed for the rest of the game. I tried to pretend I didn't see the other girls whispering and pointing at me.

"Need a ride home?" Jason asked once the game was over.

Carla walked by and she stopped to glare at me.

"Sure." I followed him and Todd out to Jason's pickup.

My house wasn't far from the school, so it didn't take long to get there. To my surprise Jason got out and walked me to the front porch. We ran to escape the rain, laughing as we splash through the mud puddles.

The roof of the porch protected us from the rain. It was coming down in buckets and I stepped back to give Jason room to get under the roof with me.

"Hey, I was wondering if you'd like to go out Saturday night."

My heart lurched. It was the first time a boy had asked me out since Jose died. I didn't know what to say.

Jason's face turned red. "If it's too soon, that's okay, I understand."

Jason is a nice guy and I liked him. It was a little soon, but I thought of how Carla treated me and found myself agreeing to go. "No, that will be fun. Thanks for asking me."

"Cool." His face brightened, and he grinned. "I'll pick you up at seven."

"Okay."

He took off back to his pickup. When he got there, he waved and jumped in. I stood on the porch watching him drive away and wondered what I'd done. Carla would never forgive me.

As soon as I got in the house, I called Patty and told her about Jason asking me out. She was really quiet for a couple minutes, then she said, "Are you sure you should? Because of...you know...Carla?"

I told her how Carla treated me at school and later at the game.

"You shouldn't go out with Jason just to get even with Carla."

I knew she was right, but there was something inside me that said I'd regret it if I didn't go out with Jason. He was one of the most popular boys at school, and he'd asked me out!

Later, after the café closed for the day my mom came home. She looked tired, so I made cream of tomato soup and grilled cheese sandwiches for us. We never wait for my father because we never knew if he was coming home or not.

"How was your day?" Mom came into the kitchen wearing her robe and slippers. She'd taken a shower to get the smell of grease out of her hair and off her skin. Her hair curled around her face. I really looked at her for the first time since all of this happened and realized her skin was white and she had dark circles under her eyes.

"It was sort of weird today." I told her how some of the girls at school acted. "I don't know why they're acting that way."

Mom sat at the table and picked up her spoon. She sipped hot soup from the spoon making soft slurping sounds. Then she put her spoon down and looked at me. "There was some talk at the café today."

I sat across from her and bit into my cheese sandwich. I closed my eyes and enjoyed the taste of the melted cheese and the homemade bread. "About what?"

Mama sighed and played with her spoon, running it back and forth on the tablecloth. "Did you tell Patty that you lied about the rape?"

My stomach sank. So, that's why I was being treated like a pariah. Patty must've told everyone she knew what I said.

Mama gave me a direct look. "Colleen, I asked you a question."

Tears filled my eyes and I bowed my head, setting my sandwich down half eaten. "Yes."

"Why?"

The kitchen was small, with only enough room for a table and chairs, but right then it seemed even smaller, like it was closing in on me.

"I meant to tell you, Mama. But the Sheriff assumed it happened, and I was so upset about Jose, and it almost did happen. If that guy hadn't come out of his house with a gun and scared them off." Sobs burst from me and I put my hand to my chest to keep it from beating through my skin.

Mama reached over and patted my hand. "It's okay, baby girl. I know you went through hell with those two and I'm so sorry. They deserve everything they get."

Her hand on mine trembled and I turned mine over and clasped hers. "Everyone in town is going to hate me now, aren't they Mama?"

She removed her hand. "No, of course they won't. There may be a few who aren't nice to you because of it, but your friends will understand."

We began to eat again when suddenly we heard, *SPLAT, SPLAT, SPLAT,* on the kitchen window. I looked over in shock and saw three globs of yellow goo sliding down the glass.

Present Day

I really enjoy my dinner with Gayle and Ben. Ben is easy going and friendly. We're sitting out on their deck drinking a glass of wine when Nick calls. I excuse myself and walk back to the guest house to talk to him. When he tells me that his wife was related to Leona, I'm amazed.

"What? How can that be?"

"Leona never mentioned that she has family in Washington?"

I think back, trying to remember. "No, I don't remember her ever mentioning any family. She told me that her parents were dead long before I came along and that she was an only child. She never had family visit or phone calls from them."

"Unless there's another Leona with ties to the Pacific Northwest, who lived in Kissimmee, Florida, it must be her. I need to call Sandi and see what she knows."

"Sandi, is that Danny's grandmother?"

"Yeah. Not that you'd know it. She never calls him either."

I hear the frustration in Nick's voice and feel bad for him and for Danny. I know that Nick wants what's best for Danny. I'm sure he'd like Liz's mom to be the type who would love her grandson, a grandmother who would call him and send gifts and have him over for a visit. It sure doesn't sound like Liz's mother is like that.

"When are you going to call her?" I ask.

"I guess right away. It would be easier than driving over there. My first thought was to get in the truck in the morning and go see her, but it's a long way."

"Where is she?"

"In Toppenish, Washington. It's about a hundred miles from here. She works at the Legends Casino. I'll give her a call. I'm sure I have her number around here somewhere."

He hangs up with the promise that he'll call me back as soon as he talks to her. I walk back outside and look around the neighborhood. It's getting dark and lights are coming on everywhere. Gayle and Ben have gone back into the house and I can see lights on in their living room.

Gayle is such an enigma to me. She can be friendly, like offering me her guest house and having me over for dinner, and she can be distant and cold. What's her story? Ben seems like a sweetheart. I wonder what it would be like to have him for a dad. Gayle said they weren't living here long when Colleen disappeared, so I know he isn't my dad, but it would be nice to find my birth father and know he's a decent person I could like. I can tell Ben's crazy about Gayle, but she sure doesn't act like it's mutual.

I run over and tap on their door. When Gayle comes to open it, I thank her for dinner and apologize for deserting them.

"That's okay. It was beginning to get chilly, so we came inside. Would you like to come in for a while?"

"Thanks, but I need to call my friend Hannah in Florida and check on her." I smile, say goodnight and head back to the cottage. Calling Hannah was an excuse. Gayle didn't act too enthused to invite me in and I'm ready to be alone to think about everything that's gone on for the last couple of days.

I wonder how Nick's doing with Liz's mother. It's killing me to wait, so I go in and turn on the television, then I turn it back off and wander around looking at the house. Gayle has put so much effort into it and it's a wonderful place.

There's a stack of home decorating magazines on the coffee table and I sit down and pick up one and flip through it. I glance at my watch and realize it has only been fifteen minutes since Nick called. I groan.

An hour later my phone rings. I slide my finger across the screen to answer knowing it's Nick.

"Hi. What did she say?"

I hear him chuckle and can't help the smile that slides across my lips. "The first time I called, she didn't take the call, so I waited a half hour and tried again. That time she did take it and I told her who I was, and she said, "I hope you don't want me to babysit or send you money, 'cause I ain't doing either one.""

"Wow! Nice lady."

"I don't think lady would describe her very well. I told her that I wanted to ask her about her aunt, Leona , and she hung up on me."

"You're kidding. Did you call back?"

"Several times." He sighs. "She wouldn't answer, so I called one of her daughters, Jodi. Out of all of them, she's the nicest. She didn't know anything about her mom's aunt, but she said she'd try and talk to Sandi and see if she can get anything out of her."

"Okay." I slip my sandals off and curl my legs up under me. "Well, thanks for trying."

"No problem. If we don't hear anything soon, I'll drive up there. It's not that far."

"Can I go with you?"

"Of course. I'll see if I can find a sitter for Danny and we'll drive up tomorrow. Hopefully, Sandi won't be able to ignore us if we're right there in her face."

I tell him about running into Helen at the grocery store. "She was actually a little nicer than every other time I've approached her."

"That's good. Helen's a nice woman. I'm surprised she doesn't want to help you."

"She said something that really got to me, Nick. She told me to look for my father. She said that maybe if I find him, I'll find Colleen."

"Do you know anything about him?"

"No. There was no father listed on either birth certificate I saw. He could be anybody. I guess I thought if I found Colleen, she'd tell me who he was."

"You'd think that if anyone knows it would be Helen."

"Yeah, you'd think so."

We talk awhile longer and hang up. I get up and put on the nightgown I bought at Wal Mart and get ready for bed. It's so quiet here. Suddenly I'm lonesome. I could call Hannah, but it's two o'clock in the morning there and I don't want to wake her. I can't help but compare tonight in this house to last night at Nick's house. I felt so happy there. Content. Here I feel all alone.

The drive to Toppenish takes about three hours. We leave around eight the next morning and get there in time for lunch at the Casino. Nick has left Danny with his grandfather. We talk so much on the way over I feel like I've known Nick forever. He tells me he hasn't dated much since Liz died. He says that he's afraid Danny will get attached and then if it doesn't work out, he'll be hurt again. I hear the warning in his voice and realize Nick is worried about our relationship, but it's for a whole different reason than why I'm worried.

Jodi calls and tells Nick that her mom has a lunch break at 11:30. We wait outside the employee entrance because Jodi said the first thing her mom does is step outside for a cigarette.

I'm shaking inside. Sandi is a relative of sorts and I'm short on relatives. The door opens, and a couple women walk out. They're wearing black pants and white shirts and I wonder if one of them is Sandi, but Nick doesn't act like he knows them, so maybe not.

When she does come out a few minutes later, Nick straightens up from where he was leaning against the building. "Sandi."

She stops and looks at us. "Shit. You don't give up, do you?"

Sandi has Danny's red hair and white skin. She has wrinkles around her eyes and mouth from too many cigarettes. She pulls a pack out of her pocket and lights up. Then she squints up at Nick. "What do you want?"

Nick looks at me and raises his eyes. "This is Natalie . She was raised by Leona."

Sandi looks over at me. "Nice to meet ya. Nick told me you're looking for your birth mother. Wish I could help, but I don't know what happened to her."

"Is there somewhere to have lunch?" Nick asks her. "I'll buy."

She sighs, takes several puffs on her cigarette and puts it out in the ashtray the casino has built near the door. "You can buy me lunch, but I have to warn you, I don't know much about Leona or why she adopted your friend."

"Maybe if we ask the right questions, you'll remember something that will help," Nick says.

She takes Nick's arm and heads for the main entrance of the casino. "There's a deli in here. We may as well eat there. It'll save time."

I can tell she's enjoying having Nick's attention. She preens when the waitress comes by the table and gives her a thumbs up. Nick looks embarrassed, and I chuckle under my breath.

Once we've ordered drinks, iced tea all around because as Sandi points out, she has to go back to work and can't have a beer, she sits back and looks at me. "So, you're Colleen's daughter."

"Did you know her?"

"I knew of her. She had quite a reputation in Cascade Locks. I was living there when she went missing."

I scoot my chair closer to the table, my heart thumping inside my chest. "Do you know what happened to her?"

Sandi shakes her head. "No, I heard that she and her sister had a fight and she left town. Then I never heard any more about her. It wasn't like we were friends. I knew who she was like everyone in Cascade Locks knew everyone else back then." She coughs, a dry hacking sound, then takes a deep breath and gazes at Nick.

"Did Leona ever say anything about adopting Natalie?" Nick takes a drink of the iced tea the waitress has set in front of him.

"Nah, it wasn't like I was close to Leona. She was quiet and reserved. She was a nurse in the Army and Mom always said she thought Leona had seen things that no woman should ever see. Mom was the talkative one. She could talk to anyone, any time. But not Leona, she pretty much kept to herself."

I nod because that was true. She was a good nurse, but she didn't talk about her patients, and I didn't know she'd been an Army nurse. In fact, I really didn't know much about her. When I went through her papers after she died, I didn't find anything about her early years. It was as if she and I both just appeared on the earth with no history behind us.

Nick continues to ask questions, trying to nudge Sandi's memory, but she shakes her head. I'm getting depressed, thinking we drove all this way for nothing. Our waitress sets our food in front of us and Sandi digs into her BLTA with gusto.

I'm picking at my salad, trying to think of some question I can ask Sandi that she might know the answer to. Finally, it hits me. "Do you know why Alice Perkins set up the adoption for Leona?"

Sandi sets her sandwich down and looks at me. "Alice Perkins. Is she still around? She must be a hundred years old."

"Not quite."

"Now there's a character. She was a cook at The Sweet Onion for years. She and Helen were thick as thieves. Maybe she did it as a favor to Helen? I doubt Helen wanted to raise Colleen's child, and if I remember right, Colleen wasn't the type to settle down and become a mother. She probably told Helen to find a family to take her kid."

My heart sinks. She seems to realize that the kid she's

talking about is me. "Sorry, Hun, I didn't mean to sound mean. I'm sure Colleen had her reasons for giving you up for adoption." She turns to Nick. "Me and my big mouth."

Nick looks at me with concern in his blue eyes.

"No, it's okay. It's not anything I don't already know."

Sandi gobbles up the rest of her sandwich and calls the waitress over. "I need to go. Got to have another cig or I won't make it through my afternoon shift." She stands up and reaches for her purse. "You don't know what these gamblers are like if they're losing, and they're usually losing."

Nick pays the bill and we follow her from the café out into the bright sunshine. I put on my sunglasses and Sandi starts to walk away. Then she turns back to Nick. "Tell the kid I said hello. I may have to come see him some day."

She raises her hand in goodbye and pulls out her cigarette pack as she walks back towards the employee entrance.

"Yeah, like I'd do that." Nick watches her, a dark scowl on his face.

On the way home, we talk about Sandi and how she doesn't want anything to do with Danny. I think about my grandmother and how she doted on me.

"Leona was a wonderful grandmother."

Nick takes his eyes off the road for a minute to smile at me. "I'm glad you have some good memories."

I look down at my hands. I've clasped them so tight, they're turning red. I try and relax. "Until I discovered her lies, I thought the world of her."

"She must've had a reason for lying to you. Maybe she was afraid Colleen would take you away from her."

"Maybe." I brush tears from my eyes. "I wish she were

here, so I could ask her. She's the one person who knows all the answers, and she died before I knew to ask."

Nick takes my hand. "We'll figure it out."

I sit for a while in silence, my head exploding with questions. Then I voice the one fear that has plagued me since I arrived in Cascade Locks. "What if she's dead?"

Nick squeezes my hand. "I'm sorry, Natalie, but you need to prepare yourself for that possibility."

I know he's right. I'm trying to convince myself that she probably is dead, but I hate the thought of that. I wanted to meet her. I wanted to know her story.

As the miles whiz by, I think about how Sandi ignores Danny. How she doesn't want to get involved in his life because she doesn't have what it takes to be a grandmother to him. Was that how Colleen felt when she found out she was pregnant with me? Did she not know what to do with a baby, so she asked her sister to find me a good home? Or was she the woman that the people in Cascade Locks knew, the one who didn't care about anyone but herself, and I was a mistake that she had to get rid of? *Or did she like the idea of the ten thousand dollars?* I try and push that thought away, but it rubs like sandpaper against my skin.

"Thank you for taking me to meet Sandi," I tell Nick as we speed down the road.

"Lot of good it did us." He puts his hand back on the steering wheel.

My fingers tingle from the feel of his skin against mine. "Well, we know two things we didn't know before we went."

Nick glances over at me. "What's that? I didn't think she came up with anything that would help."

I smile. "We know that Helen and Alice were once

thick as thieves as Sandi put it. That's something I didn't know. And we know that they must've had some sort of falling out or they'd still be friends." I sit back and cross my arms over my stomach. "Now we just have to get one of them to tell us what happened." As if that would be easy.

CHAPTER 27: NATALIE

Present Day

After Nick drops me off at the guest house with a promise of dinner soon, I think about what my next step is. I'd love to spend the evening with Nick and Danny, but I sense that Nick is taking a step back, not wanting to get involved because of Danny. I understand that I'll be leaving Cascade Locks soon and I don't want to hurt him either.

But maybe we're related. If not through Nick, which I hope with all my heart we're not, then through Leona and Liz. If that's true, it would give me a good excuse to keep in touch with Danny no matter what. I like that idea.

The next morning, I call the sheriff's office again and ask to speak to Sheriff Anderson. He comes on the phone and I tell him who I am.

"Funny, I was just going to call you. Have you remembered anything that you had in your room at the hotel that the arsonist would not want seen?"

"The only thing is a picture I had of Colleen Winters. I can't imagine burning down a hotel just to eliminate a picture."

"No, I can't either."

"So, that makes me think he's trying to scare me off. Probably because he doesn't want me to find out what happened to my mother."

I can hear his chair squeak as he leans back in it. "Well, that's possible."

"I heard you lived in Cascade Locks back when my mother went missing. Did you know Colleen?"

There's silence on the other end of the phone for a couple of minutes. The chair squeaks again and his voice is deep when he says, "yeah, I knew her. Lots of men knew her."

My stomach dips, but I let that slide. "Do you know what happened to her?"

"No. I wish I did. She went missing and we all thought she'd left town. But I can see now that we should have tried harder to find her."

"No one turned her in as missing?"

"Not that I'm aware of. It's like one day she was there and the next she was gone. She was hell bent on making folks' life miserable, I just thought she got tired of the game and moved on."

"Was she that terrible?"

He's silent for a long time and when he speaks his voice has softened. "Not always. Before that boyfriend of hers was murdered, she was a cute little thing. Her mother taught her to be respectful and kind. The town taught her to be angry."

While I'm digesting that, he says he's got a call coming in he needs to take, and he's gone. So, Colleen's boyfriend was murdered. Who was he? Maybe that's why she was so miserable and tried to make everyone else miserable, too. I need to talk to Alice.

I drive into town and park at the grocery and then walk over to Alice's house. I feel like I'm beating my head against a brick wall, but I've got to make her and Helen talk to me. I know they have the key to what happened to my mother.

Alice's voice hollers a feeble "Come in." when I knock on her door. I remember to lift it up to open it and walk in. She's sitting in the same exact spot that she was the last time I visited. In fact, I think she's wearing the same clothes. Dirty navy-blue pants and a floral top that don't match.

She raises her head with an expectant look on her face. "Oh, it's you."

"Yeah, it's me. Are you expecting company?"

She shrugs. "Got a friend bringing me food every day about this time."

I sit on her sofa, doing my best not to touch anything. Today she has a window open and it's not quite as awful in here as it was last time I came. "I need you to tell me about Colleen. I just talked to the sheriff and he said she wasn't a bad girl until her boyfriend was killed. You mentioned before that she was involved with a Mexican boy. What happened?"

Alice's mouth tightens. "I couldn't say."

Can't or won't? There's a picture of a little blond hair boy on the end table next to her. I point to it. "Is that your son?"

Alice nods. "He was such a good boy."

"What happened to him?" I'm whispering, almost like we're in church, and I don't know why, but it seems the right thing to do.

She's looking at me, but not seeing me. Hate burns in her eyes and I shiver, suddenly afraid of this tiny old woman, which is crazy because she's so frail, there's nothing she could do to me. "What happened to your son?"

Tears run down her cheeks. "He was killed in prison."

"I'm so sorry."

"He shouldn't have gone there. It was your mother who put him there. Her with her lies and her crazy talk. She should've been locked up. Not my boy." She struggles to stand and almost topples over.

I get up and move away from her, not knowing what she intends. "I knew that Colleen was bad news. Told my Stevie to stay away from her, but he wouldn't have it. He kept on wanting her, even when she was screwing that Mexican boy."

She starts towards me and I see what looks like a knife in her hand. Then she yells at me. "Get out of my house and don't you ever come back, you hear me? I don't want the likes of you around here."

I back up towards the door, not taking my eyes off her. The door opens behind me and I breathe a sigh of relief. I turn around to see who it is, and I'm glad to see Gayle standing there. She has a casserole dish in her hand and a basket hanging from her arm.

"What's going on?"

"She was just leaving." Alice points to me.

"She thinks my mother lied to the police and they put her son in jail for killing a Mexican boy."

Gayle takes a deep breath. "What?"

"It's the truth." There's a murderous glint in Alice's eyes. "She lied about everything. And now my Stevie is dead and it's all her fault."

She advances towards me and Gayle steps between us. "It's not Natalie's fault, Alice. Colleen left a long time ago, remember?"

Alice blinks and looks at me. "You look so much like her." She slowly makes her way back to her chair. There's a stack of unopened bills on the end table next to her, and that's when I realize that what I thought was a knife is really a letter opener. My heartbeat slows down a bit.

"Go back to the house," Gayle tells me. "I'll be there soon."

I nod and walk out the door. My hands are shaking as I pull my phone out of my purse. I hate to call Nick, but I don't know what else to do. When he answers, I ask him to please meet me at Gayle's. My voice shakes and he doesn't ask questions just says he'll be there.